PUZZLED

Indemnity

Also by Parnell Hall

NYPD Puzzle

Arsenic and Old Puzzles

$10,000 in Small, Unmarked Puzzles

The KenKen Killings

The Puzzle Lady vs. the Sudoku Lady

Dead Man's Puzzle

You Have the Right to Remain Puzzled

Stalking the Puzzle Lady

And a Puzzle to Die On

With This Puzzle, I Thee Kill

A Puzzle in a Pear Tree

Puzzled to Death

Last Puzzle & Testament

A Clue for the Puzzle Lady

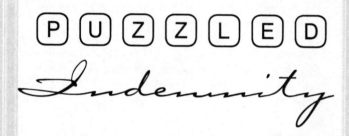

PUZZLED Indemnity

A Puzzle Lady Mystery

Parnell Hall

MINOTAUR BOOKS
A THOMAS DUNNE BOOK
New York

A THOMAS DUNNE BOOK FOR MINOTAUR BOOKS.
An imprint of St. Martin's Publishing Group.

www.thomasdunnebooks.com
www.minotaurbooks.com

Library of Congress Cataloging-in-Publication Data

Hall, Parnell.
Puzzled indemnity : a Puzzle Lady mystery / Parnell Hall. — First edition.
        pages ; cm. — (Puzzle lady mysteries ; 14)
    ISBN 978-1-250-02717-7 (hardcover)
    ISBN 978-1-250-02718-4 (e-book)
  1. Felton, Cora (Fictitious character)—Fiction.   I. Title.
    PS3558.A37327P795 2015
    813'.54—dc23

                                            2014032398

Minotaur books may be purchased for educational, business, or promotional use. For information on bulk purchases, please contact the Macmillan Corporate and Premium Sales Department at 1-800-221-7945, extension 5442, or write to special markets@macmillan.com.

First Edition: January 2015

10 9 8 7 6 5 4 3 2 1

For my wife,
who hasn't killed me yet

Double Indemnity

I have taken out insurance against my ineptness and lack of expertise by enlisting the help of two of the finest puzzle constructors in the field:

New York Times crossword editor Will Shortz created the sudoku, and frequent *New York Times* contributor Fred Piscop created the crosswords.

And I have doubled my coverage by prevailing upon American Crossword Puzzle Tournament champion Ellen Ripstein to edit them.

These people ensure me against my own folly.

I cannot thank them enough.

PUZZLED

Indemnity

Chapter

1

Cora Felton looked out the window and proclaimed, "I hate winter."

"That's nothing new," Sherry Carter said. "You also hate spring, summer, and fall. They're too hot, too wet, too windy, as I recall. Though not in that order."

"What, you thought I was going to call you on your wordplay? Let's remember who's the cruciverbalist here."

The cruciverbalist was Sherry. Cora, the Puzzle Lady, whose crossword puzzle column was nationally syndicated and who hawked breakfast cereal to schoolchildren on TV, was merely a front for her niece. Cora hated crossword puzzles, largely because she couldn't solve them and people were always asking her to because they thought she could. This tended to make Cora cranky regardless of the season.

At the moment there was no puzzle on the horizon, only snow.

"Now is the winter of our discontent," Cora said.

"*Richard III*? You're quoting *Richard III*?"

"Hey, I've been to the theater."

"Yeah, but Shakespeare?"

"It's the first line of the play. I didn't fall asleep till five minutes in."

Sherry shook her head. "Cora, why must you always pretend to be less educated than you are?"

"Give me a break. I'm the goddamned Puzzle Lady. I'm always pretending to be *more* educated than I am. It's exhausting, feigning an expertise you do not have. You know what a relief it is to let my hair down and be lowbrow?"

"Nonsense," Sherry said. "You do that all day long. You delight in shocking people with your earthy, just-one-of-the-guys approach to everything. It's only when the topic turns to crosswords you go into your shell."

On the front lawn, Sherry's daughter, Jennifer, was loping through the snow in large, happy circles. Buddy the toy poodle cavorted along behind. Every now and then an ear or the tip of his tail could be seen over the top of the snow.

"I should charge you a babysitting fee," Cora said.

"I should charge you a dog-walking fee. Aren't you glad Buddy has a playmate?"

"I'm glad he doesn't expect me to play in the snow."

"No, only Jennifer expects that."

"I'm a city girl, born and bred. Snow is that white stuff you can't go out until doormen shovel off the sidewalk."

"You're going to hole up inside the house until it melts?"

"That's a depressing thought."

"Everything's a depressing thought for you these days. You've been in a funk ever since you broke up with the policeman."

"We didn't break up. We live in different places. When I'm in New York I call him up."

"And when he's in Bakerhaven?"

"Hell has frozen over. He's a New York City cop. What would he be doing in Bakerhaven?"

Jennifer fell on her face. She stood up, plastered with snow from head to foot, and immediately started bawling.

"Guess I have to go get her," Sherry said.

"You have to get her anyway. Here comes the snowplow."

"Again? They were here yesterday."

"They're desperate for the work," Cora said. "It's all this global warming."

Sherry pulled on a jacket and boots. "Aren't you going to get Buddy?"

"Don't have to. He'll follow you."

Cora watched through the window as Sherry went out to rescue her child.

Jennifer stopped crying the minute Sherry picked her up, but protested mightily when Mommy started carrying her toward the door. She might have fallen on her face and got snow down the neck of her snowsuit, but that didn't mean she wanted to come *in*.

As Cora predicted, Buddy stayed with Jennifer, safely out of range of the blades of the snowplow. Even so, she should have gone out. She was getting lazy and complacent.

Something needed to be done.

"I need a job."

Becky Baldwin pushed the long blond hair out of her eyes and looked up at Cora Felton. "You know how many years we've been working together?"

Cora made a face. "Do you know what an annoying question that is for someone as young as you to ask someone as old as me?"

Becky smiled. "That wasn't the point I was going for, though it certainly is an amusing perk. It's just in all the time I've known you I don't think you ever asked me for a job."

"Really? I've asked Chief Harper."

"How'd that work out for you?"

"I got arrested for murder."

"Well, I wouldn't blame the chief. That happens when you work for me, too. Rather recently, as I recall."

"So you don't have anything?"

"Why do you want a job?"

"I'm bouncing off the walls. It's winter, and I'm stir-crazy. I'm snowed in with a mother and a two-year-old. Not that the kid's not cute as a button. But you like your children in small doses. That's the joy of being an aunt. It's not your kid, so it's not full-time."

"So that's why you want a job?"

"Wouldn't you?"

"I *have* a job."

"My point exactly."

"Not even close. I have to work because I need the money. People *give* you money for being the Puzzle Lady."

"It does seem unfair, doesn't it?"

"Yeah, well, if you want a job you've come to the wrong place. I don't have anything at the moment."

"You don't have any clients?"

"I don't have any clients who need your services."

"You have any clients who don't need my services?"

Becky cocked her head. "Are you *trying* to be annoying?"

Cora smiled. "Don't like it, do you? I was cross-examining you, like a lawyer would. Part of my new drive to turn the tables on the professionals. Like giving doctors a dosage of their own medication."

"Huh?"

"You know, when a doctor tries to snow you with medical jargon, puffing up words with extra syllables to make them seem more important. 'Dose' becomes 'dosage.' 'Medicine' becomes 'medication.' "

"You're concerned with copyright infringement?"

"Huh?"

"You're the wordsmith. If anyone's going to be snowing people with fancy language it ought to be you."

Becky was one of two people who knew Cora couldn't solve crosswords but still thought she created them. The other was Harvey Beerbaum, Bakerhaven's resident cruciverbalist. Cora had been forced to tell Harvey she couldn't solve puzzles to get him to help her when Sherry was in the hospital having Jennifer. Which, Cora realized, was actually before she had to tell Becky. Keeping track of who knew what and when did they know it was only slightly less complicated than Watergate, yet another reason for Cora to hate crosswords.

"Yeah, that's it," Cora said. She dropped the snappy banter, sank into a chair.

Becky frowned. "Cora. What's wrong?"

Cora sighed. "I haven't seen Crowley in months."

"Ah. Man trouble. I might have known."

"You needn't sound so happy about it."

"Well, you always took delight in my man trouble. Even went so far as to create some."

Without actually saying so, Cora had managed to leave the impression Becky was running around with a married man.

"I don't know *how* those rumors got started."

"I'm sorry you're having problems with the sergeant. Why don't you go to New York and work it out?"

"I can't go running off and leave Sherry snowed in with a kid."

"She's not snowed in."

"She might as well be. If I've got the car, she can't go anywhere."

"Don't you have the car now?"

"It's not the same thing. I'm only ten minutes away."

"Yeah, if you had a cell phone. How's she going to reach you?"

"She calls you or she calls Chief Harper. It's not that big a town." Cora waved it away. "Whatever. The point is, I'm not running off to New York. You really don't have any work?"

Becky shook her head. "Better ask the chief."

Cora found Chief Harper sitting on the floor of his office banging on the radiator with a monkey wrench.

"I'm not sure that's the way that tool was intended to be used, Chief."

"Oh, yeah?" Harper said. "Well, I tried loosening the valve that holds the steam back and guess what? No steam."

"The police department didn't pay the bill?"

"Very funny. The furnace is on the pipes are hot, Dan's got heat in the outer office. The only place that's cold is here."

"How about the holding cells?"

"No one's complained."

"Anyone in them?"

"Not that I know of. It's been a slow week." Harper gave the radiator valve another whack with the wrench.

"Why don't you buy yourself an electric space heater?"

"Why should I have to lay out the money?"

"Can't the police department buy it?"

"Sure, if I want to be investigated for graft and corruption."

"It can't be as bad as all that."

"You'd be surprised. I'm safer calling a plumber."

"Won't a plumber cost a lot more than a heater?"

"Sure, but it's maintenance. No one's going to fault me for that." Harper clambered to his feet, plopped himself into his desk chair. It squeaked a little. The chief had put on weight. "So, what brings you by my chilly office?"

"I just dropped in to see what's shaking. I didn't realize business was so slow."

"I think it's the cold weather," Harper said. "The troublemakers stay home."

"Don't people pack the bars and get rowdy?"

"Sure, and we lock 'em up overnight and send 'em home the next day. If we're strapped for cash, we let 'em stop by the courthouse and pay a fine."

"That's pretty cynical, Chief. What brought this on?"

"I don't know. Working with your homicide sergeant last summer kind of pointed up the inadequacies of the department."

"He's not my homicide sergeant."

"Oh? You could have fooled me."

"Come on, Chief. For a small-town police department, you've certainly had your share of murders. Hell, it's like living in Cabot Cove."

"I'll give you that," Harper said. "It's just the NYPD has cases every day. We haven't had one since last summer."

"Well, I'll put out the word, see what I can drum up."

"So how's the family? How's that cute niece of yours?" Harper flushed. "Grandniece, I mean."

"It's all right, Chief. I won't tell your wife you think Sherry Carter's cute."

"You know what I mean. It's just a pain to say 'grandniece.' I'm not even sure it's a word; is it?"

Cora, of course, had no idea. But that was the type of Puzzle Lady question she had no problem sidestepping. "I could care less whether it's a word; the fact is I don't like it. 'Grandniece' sounds too much like 'grandmother,' which sounds too much like 'doddering old fool one step away from the junk heap.'" Cora put up her hands. "Please, do not quote me on that to my adoring public. I have nothing but respect for senior citizens. I just don't happen to want to *be* one. Anyway, she's a little dickens, bright as a button, too cute for her own good."

"How old is she?"

Cora made a face. "It always comes back to age. She's two. Two something, if you're an obsessive parent who deals in months. As far as I'm concerned she's two. At some point they'll tell me she's two and a half, so that's what I'll say. How's your family?" she added a little belatedly.

"Clara's fine," Harper said. "Not that we know much about it. She's in Boston, working as a teacher's assistant at BU. I gather she's got a boyfriend, most likely undesirable, since she won't tell us anything about him. We have to keep reassuring each other she's old enough to take care of herself."

Cora was damned if she was going to ask how old Chief Harper's daughter was. There were some things she just didn't want to know. She sighed. "Aw, gee, Chief. Things really are slow. I actually stopped by to see if you had anything for me. I can see you don't."

"Oh. Now that you mention it, I do have something for you."

"Oh?"

"Yeah. Hang on. I got it right here."

Harper pulled open the top drawer of her desk, reached in, and took out a piece of paper. He looked at it, handed it to Cora.

It was a crossword puzzle.

Across

1 "Famous" cookie maker
5 Utter hoarsely
9 Monk's monotone
14 Gaucho's cow-catcher
15 Epps of TV's "House"
16 Sports artist Neiman
17 Start of a message
19 All fired up
20 Lady of Spain
21 Salad green
23 Tutor in Siam
25 Neutral hue
26 Oracles' signs
29 More of the message
35 Tacit assent
36 Comparison word
38 Precede, with "to"
39 "Animal House" attire
41 Make a toast, say
43 An Ephron
44 Ark terminus
46 Fat for cooking

48 VCR's "go back"
49 More of the message
51 Ruhr industrial hub
53 Links stat
54 A pop
56 North Carolina cape
61 "Because I __!"
   (response to "Why?")
65 Earthy pigment
66 End of the message
68 Impish looks
69 Creator of Bunker and
   Stivic
70 Amphitheater shape
71 Have a feeling
72 Old U.S. gas brand
73 White-hatted cowboy,
   stereotypically

Down

1 Basics
2 Oliver Twist's request
3 Big name in chemicals
4 Apia native
5 Atkinson of "Mr. Bean"
6 "Do no harm" org.
7 Command under "File"
   in Word
8 Magician's word
9 Scrub down
10 Judge, as a case
11 Affleck film set in Iran

12 Yule tune
13 Radial on a Rolls
18 __ & Young (accounting
   firm)
22 Talk-radio contributor
24 Way, way off
26 Like draft beer
27 Roger who played Bond
28 Mystery writer's award
30 __ fours (crawling)
31 1/24 of a case
32 Dumpster emanations
33 Make into mush
34 Reproduce like salmon
37 Armed conflict
40 Dadaist Jean
42 Chess move signified by
   an "x"
45 Impugn the character of
47 "Unleaded" java
50 Good for farming
52 Civil War battle of 1862
55 American Leaguer as of 2013
56 Takes most of
57 Zoning unit
58 Like a beanpole
59 Sawbucks
60 Drags to court
62 Olive-branch bearer
63 Train in the ring
64 Capital on a fjord
67 Carrier to 64-Down

Chapter

4

Cora's heart sank. This was the kind of Puzzle Lady problem she could not easily sidestep. Her mind began racing to see what type of subterfuge she could employ to avoid having to solve the damn thing, the odds of which happening were somewhere in the neighborhood of a million to none. The problem with her excuses was she had used them all so often it was getting ridiculous, sort of like how many times will it take Lois Lane to realize Clark Kent ducks out every time Superman appears?

Cora had never solved a crossword puzzle in front of anyone, and it was a miracle this fact had managed to escape notice. The saving grace was sudoku. Cora was as good at number puzzles as she was bad at crosswords and whizzed through sudoku with a speed unparalleled by even the likes of Harvey Beerbaum, who fancied himself an expert. Cora solved sudoku with ease in the presence of Chief Harper, though, so as not to make him suspicious, only after her ritual feigned reluctance.

There was nothing feigned about her reluctance now.

"Oh, for goodness' sakes," Cora said. "I can't believe you're giving me a crossword puzzle. Don't I ever get a day off? I'm the Puzzle Lady, so I'm always on call?"

"I thought you were looking for work."

"*Police* work. Not this crap. Give me a crime scene to inspect. A suspect to interview. A clue to interpret." Cora pointed at the crossword. "And don't tell me that's a clue. That's a pain in the fanny. Boring, boring, boring. Dreamed up by someone to take the fun out of life."

Chief Harper put up his hands. "Relax, relax. No one's asking you to do anything. You weren't here, so I had Dan run this over to Harvey Beerbaum."

"Oh, really," Cora said, mollified. "Where did it come from?"

"It was in the morning mail."

"I assume if there was a return address we wouldn't be having this conversation."

"There was no return address."

"Where was it postmarked?"

"Here in Bakerhaven."

"Can I see it?"

"Why?"

"You can learn a lot from an envelope."

"You don't want to see the puzzle, but you want to see the envelope?"

"Why not? I'm not the Envelope Lady. I won't feel like a doctor at a cocktail party having to listen to everybody's symptoms."

Harper took an envelope out of the drawer, passed it over.

"You handled it?"

"Sure."

"You didn't process it for fingerprints?"

"Why should I? There hasn't been a crime."

"There will be in a minute. You get an anonymous letter with a crossword puzzle in it and you think it important enough to rush it over to Harvey Beerbaum."

"You'd rather I waited for you?"

"God, no. All anonymous crossword puzzles should go straight to Harvey Beerbaum. It gives him something to do."

There came the sound of a door in the outer office.

"Dan's back," Harper said. "You mind taking a look at the solved puzzle?"

"That I can handle," Cora said. "Though if there's anything to it, I'm sure Harvey found it."

"The puzzle, yeah. He doesn't always apply it to the situation."

"There *is* no situation. It's just a puzzle."

Dan Finley came in the door. The young officer was a Puzzle Lady fan, had heard of Cora Felton even before he met her. For Chief Harper, on the other hand, it had been news that there even was a Puzzle Lady.

"Got it, Chief. Hi, Cora. You here to look at the puzzle?"

"No, but I guess that's what I'm going to do. What's it all about?"

Dan grinned. "You want *me* to tell *you* what this puzzle means?"

"Well, you have the advantage of having seen it."

"Oh. There was a copy here. Didn't you give her the copy, Chief?"

"He gave me the copy, but I didn't want to solve it and steal Harvey Beerbaum's thunder. What'd he come up with?"

"Here you go."

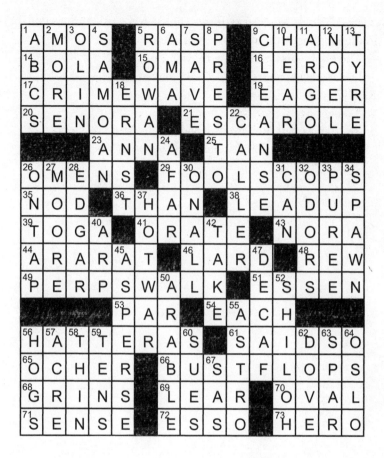

Cora took the puzzle and read the theme entry:

Crime wave fools cops. Perps walk. Bust flops.

"Well, Chief, this is the type of taunting message a sadistic serial killer would use to make you feel small and helpless. Not that you are, of course. I'm just saying that would be the intent."

"Small and helpless about what? Not knowing what the guy

means? I think whoever sent this should feel small and useless for not having made the slightest impression."

The phone on Chief Harper's desk rang.

Dan Finley scooped it up. "Bakerhaven police. . . . Uh-huh. . . . Really? . . . Be right there."

"What have we got?" Harper said.

"Ed James, out on Tyson's Road. Liquor store robbery."

Cora rubbed her hands together. "Well, that's more like it."

Chapter

[5]

It was quite a while since Cora had been in a liquor store, having quit drinking, but from what she recalled of Ed James Wine and Spirits what was surprising was not that it had been robbed, but that it had not been robbed more often. The store occupied its own mini-mall, fronted by a rectangular parking lot twice as wide as the storefront and boasting enough paint-lined parking spaces to give one the impression that all anyone ever did in Connecticut was drink. Having once fallen into that category, Cora was not one to point fingers; still the size of the lot seemed excessive. At the moment there were only four cars in it. Two were police cruisers, one was hers, and the other presumably belonged to the owner.

Ed James had a slender face, thinning gray hair, slightly long, a gray mustache, and suspicious eyes, as if from years of seriously doubting the ID card you had produced to show you were twenty-one was in fact genuine.

Chief Harper took the lead. "So, Ed, Dan says you've been robbed."

Ed nodded. "That's right. At gunpoint," he added. He seemed somewhat pleased by the assertion.

"So, who did it?"

"Well now, that's why I called you."

"Yes, but I didn't see the robber. I'm assuming you did."

"I did, for all the good it's going to do you. The guy wore a mask."

"A mask," Dan Finley said. "You mean like the Wild West?"

Harper gave him a look.

"No," Ed said. "Not a bandana. Not a stocking, either. I mean a Halloween mask."

"A plastic mask?" Harper said.

"It had plastic in it. But not the kind held on with an elastic band. This covered the whole head."

"You mean a hood?" Cora said.

"That's right, a hood. But the face was plastic."

"And who *was* the face?" Harper said.

"Oh. Iron Man. You know, the superhero."

Cora's eyes twinkled. "You got robbed by one of the Avengers?"

Ed James fixed her with a baleful eye. "I don't find it amusing. I was robbed."

"What did the guy get?" Harper said.

"Cash. Cleaned out the register."

"How much was that?"

"Not much. Not that many people use cash these days."

"When you say 'not much'?"

"Oh, five or six hundred dollars. Not chicken feed, but if it weren't for credit cards it'd be much worse."

"Dan said you couldn't describe the car."

"That's right."

"How come?"

"Didn't see a car. Parking lot was empty."

"There was no one in the store?"

"No. Just me and him. The only car in the parking lot was mine."

"So he left on foot?"

"That's right. Ran out the door, went into the woods."

"Which way?"

"Back toward town."

"So what did the guy look like?" Harper said. "Big, small?"

Cora knew the answer before Ed said it.

"Average size. In a blue overcoat. L.L. Bean, from the look of it. No hat, just the hood."

"Gloves?"

"No."

"He touch anything? The register?"

"No. He made me clean it out."

"How long was he here?"

"Not long. It all happened fast. I had a customer. Customer left. He must have been waiting outside. As soon as the customer drove off, he came in. Mask on, gun out. Said, 'Keep your hands where I can see 'em.' "

"What was his voice like?"

"Low and raspy, like he was disguising it."

"He say anything else?"

"He said, 'Empty the register.' He took a paper bag out of his jacket pocket, opened it, set it on the counter."

"He say anything then?"

"He didn't have to. Just gestured with his gun. I put the money in the bag; he picked it up and went out."

Chief Harper asked a few more questions, but Ed James wasn't much help.

"Poor guy," Dan Finley said as they walked back to their cars. "When you get robbed by Iron Man, that's a pretty bad day."

"Could have been worse," Cora said.

"How's that?"

"Could have been the Incredible Hulk."

Chapter

6

The woman was ridiculously young. Becky Baldwin thought so, and most people considered Becky Baldwin ridiculously young. Most people in the legal profession, at any rate. Which wasn't fair. Becky wasn't that young anymore; she just looked young, mostly because she was so dazzlingly beautiful she would not have looked out of place on the cover of a Victoria's Secret catalogue.

The woman in the client's chair made her look like Whistler's mother.

The girl—Becky couldn't help thinking of her as a girl—was a baby-faced blonde with a look of wide-eyed innocence, her eyebrows slightly raised and her lips slightly parted as if in surprise to discover this newly voluptuous figure was in fact hers. It was a look men would find irresistible, women infuriating.

Becky couldn't afford to be infuriated. Times were tough. This was a potential client. She smiled. "And what may I do for you?"

"I need your help."

"I assumed you did. Otherwise, what would be the point?"

"Huh?"

"People who consult lawyers need help. What do you need help with?"

The young woman took a breath. Her sweater swelled dramatically. "It's my husband."

Becky blinked. The woman had a husband? She looked barely old enough to begin dating. "What's his name? What's yours, for that matter?"

"Oh, I'm sorry. I'm just new at this. I'm Brittany Wells. My husband is Hank. Hank Wells."

"How long have you been married?"

"We were married in June."

That was good. If the woman had said "ten years," Becky would have felt eligible for AARP.

"And you're having trouble with your husband?"

"I'm not sure."

Becky smiled, but it was all she could do to keep her teeth from grinding. There were limits to how long she was going to indulge this ditsy young woman. She wondered if she would be more tolerant if Brittany were scatterbrained and elderly.

"What makes you think you might have a problem with your husband?"

Brittany swallowed, blinked her eyes, blurted out, "I think he might be seeing someone else," and dissolved into tears.

Becky couldn't help a certain satisfaction. Golden Girl's fairytale existence wasn't all happily ever after. "Do you know who?"

"No."

"Then what makes you think he is?"

Brittany snuffled, said, "He's been staying late after work."

"Do you think it's his secretary?"

Brittany looked shocked. "What makes you say that?"

"It often is."

"But . . ."

"But what?"

"Hank doesn't have a secretary."

Becky closed her eyes, opened them. Said dryly, "That would seem to rule that out. Do you have any idea who the woman is?"

"No."

"Well, give me some help here. You say he stays late after work. How late?"

"Sometimes he doesn't get home till ten."

"Really? Where does he say he's been?"

"Working."

"What does he do?"

"He's an insurance salesman."

"In Bakerhaven?"

"No, in New York."

"He commutes to the City?"

"Yes."

"Oh."

"Why do you say 'oh'?"

"Well, it certainly changes the complexion. If he were working in Bakerhaven, ten o'clock would be outrageous. If he's commuting from Manhattan, it's different. What time does he get home usually?"

"Seven or eight."

"That makes the whole thing reasonable. If he had extra work to do, eight o'clock could easily stretch to ten. I'm not sure you have a problem."

"You don't understand."

"I'm trying to understand. You gotta give me something more to go on."

"When we got married he was loving, sweet. Demanding, even. Now he's not so . . . attentive."

"You can't expect him to be. The honeymoon is over. He's had to go back to work."

"Hey, whose side are you on?"

"Yours, of course. If you hire me. I'm not sure what you want me to do."

"I can't live with doubt."

"Of course not. So you want to know if your husband's having an affair."

"Yes."

"If he is, you want me to handle the divorce?"

Her lip trembled again. "I don't want a divorce."

"You want your husband."

"Yes."

"So the ideal outcome would be if you were mistaken. If he really was working late at the office."

"I suppose."

"Well, there's one way to find out. Have someone follow him when he leaves work."

"You mean like a private detective?"

"That's right."

"I don't know any private detectives."

"You didn't know me, either."

"Huh?"

"You want to hire me. What's the difference?"

"You're in the yellow pages. Under 'Attorneys.' There isn't any listing for private detectives."

"You looked up 'Private Detectives'?"

"I didn't know what to do. I looked up everything. Then I thought of attorneys."

"Mrs. Wells," Becky said. She almost stumbled over the word "Mrs." "If your husband works in Manhattan, why not hire a private investigator from Manhattan?"

"I'm not going to hire him on the phone. That would be silly. How could I give him Hank's picture?"

Becky frowned.

"Can't *you* hire me a detective?"

"I could, but you'd have to hire me to do it. If your husband isn't cheating—which we're hoping to find—you'll have hired both of us for no reason."

"What do you mean, 'no reason'? If it gives me peace of mind."

"Yes, and a detective can do that. But you don't need me. Hire a detective to make an investigation. If there's nothing wrong, you're done. If something *is* wrong, then you come to me. The way things stand, I wouldn't feel right taking your money. And don't let this small office over the pizza parlor fool you; I don't come cheap. If you need me, I'm worth it. But right now there's nothing for me to do."

Brittany took a breath. "What about the insurance policy?"

"What insurance policy?"

"My husband took out an insurance policy. That's what got me thinking in the first place. That there might be someone else."

"Hold on a minute," Becky said. "You mean a life insurance policy?"

"That's right."

"When did he do that?"

"A couple of months ago. And it was one of those policies that pay more for an accident."

"Double indemnity?"

"That's it."

"How much was it for?"

"A million dollars. Two million for an accident."

Becky smiled. "Maybe there *is* something I can do for you."

Cora stuck her head in the door. "You wanted to see me?"

"Yes, I do," Becky said. "How'd you know?"

"You called the police station."

"You don't have a cell phone. The only way I can get you is call around."

"I was busy. Chief Harper has a case."

"Really? Anything in it for me?"

"Not unless he arrests someone. Which isn't likely."

"I'll tell him you said that."

"It's armed robbery. The liquor store out on Tyson's Road. The cops haven't got a clue."

"In an armed robbery? They didn't get a description of the robber?"

"Actually, they did. The guy looked like Robert Downey Jr."

"Well, what more do you need?"

"That's Robert Downey Jr. in the Avengers movie."

"I didn't see it."

"He was Iron Man."

"Oh."

"You should get out more. Anyway, the cops got nothing. And not for lack of trying. They're canvassing every costume shop within a hundred miles."

"Are there many?"

"More than you'd think. That includes Manhattan. And there's party stores, and costume stores, and costume party stores, and Halloween costume party stores. You can also buy the damn things online. It's doubtful a robber did that, 'cause he'd leave a paper trail, but they gotta check it. Dan's going nuts tracing online purchases. Apparently, there's all kinds of Iron Man costumes and the liquor store owner can't identify the one the guy was wearing. Can you imagine that police lineup?" Cora chuckled at the thought.

"So what are you doing on the case?"

"Making helpful suggestions. That's the joy of being an unpaid consultant. You can sit back and sharp shoot. I say, 'Gee, I wonder if there's been any similar armed robberies lately.' And then Dan has to check on it."

"I thought he was canvassing costume stores."

"Dan's a great multitasker. I admire his work ethic. I wouldn't want it, but I admire it in others."

"That's hardly the sort of thing a prospective employer wants to hear."

"You have a job for me?"

"Well, I did. But from what you say, I'd be better off hiring Dan Finley."

"Don't be a wiseass. What's the job?"

Becky gave Cora a rundown of the Brittany Wells situation.

"Wow," Cora said. "Married less than a year and he's ready to dump her already?"

"Not dump her. Cash her in for the insurance."

"What's she like?"

Becky considered. "You know how you hated all Melvin's girl-friends?"

Cora's ex-husband Melvin was a thorn in her side. Since the divorce, he'd managed to drive her crazy with his parade of adolescent bimbos.

"I seem to remember them," Cora said.

"Think younger."

"A preschooler? I thought there were laws."

"There should be. Anyway, this girl isn't as bright as a preschooler, but she managed to figure out a double-indemnity life insurance policy plus her husband working late at the office all the time just might spell trouble."

"You want to hire me to check it out?"

"You got it."

"I assume you want me to tail the husband when he leaves work and see who he's shacking up with."

"That's right."

"Okay. Where's he work?"

"That's the icing on the cake."

Cora frowned. "Oh?"

Becky grinned. "New York City."

Chapter

8

Cora hit town at three thirty. For once she wished she had a cell phone. Instead she had to cruise around until she found a pay phone. Not to mention a parking spot. A working pay phone and a legal parking spot was a long-shot parlay. Cora couldn't even tell what *was* a parking spot anymore, because there weren't any parking meters; there was one Muni-Meter per block that sold slips of paper you placed on your windshield to tell the meter maid how much time you had in the hope that the place you were parked actually was legal. Cora hated the Muni-Meter. She was always afraid she would get a ticket while she was on her way to buy the parking slip. Not that she'd pay the fine, she'd fight it to her dying breath, but it would mean wasting a day in court.

Cora got lucky. The parking spot she spotted half a block away was still there when the light changed, the Muni-Meter spit out the parking slip, and the pay phone on the corner actually worked.

Cora punched in the number. She was amazed she remembered it after so many months.

Two rings, and a gruff voice growled, "Crowley."

"Wow. You always answer the phone like that, or are you expecting a call from a shyster?"

A pause. "Cora?"

"Yeah."

"It's been a while. What are you up to?"

"I'm in town."

"Really? What brings you here?"

"Well, it's not your charming demeanor. I got a job."

"Doing what?"

"Tailing a cheating husband."

"Like in the movies."

"Do they do that in the movies?"

"They used to. I haven't been lately."

"Oh? Whaddya do for fun?"

"Catch bad guys."

"I thought that's what you did for work."

"Maybe. I get confused." There was a pause. "So your case. Anything I can help you with?"

"Wanna sit on stakeout?"

"Little out of my line. I mean more like running license plates and pulling rap sheets."

"I'm not there yet."

"Well, call me when you are." Another pause. "I don't suppose you got time to stop up now."

"I gotta scout the stakeout."

"Figured. You using your car?"

"Got to. The guy's from Bakerhaven."

"Yeah, but if he's shackin' up in town . . ."

"I don't know that he is. He could be driving back to Bakerhaven, shackin' up a mile from his house."

"Yeah, but what if he's not? You may have to follow him on foot."

"I know. How are you at fixing parking tickets?"

"What, a homicide sergeant squaring a parking ticket? For the famous Puzzle Lady, no less. There's one way to make Page Six of the *New York Post*."

"I could show you another."

"I bet you could." His chuckle sounded a bit forced. "Look, I have to work. Call me if you need me."

Cora hung up the phone with nerveless fingers. She had envisioned many ways the conversation might go, and this was not one of them. Well, it was, but it wasn't on her Top Ten List. It was on her list of Outcomes So Odious as to Be Beneath Consideration.

It could not have been a colder conversation. After all they'd meant to each other. Well, after all he'd meant to her. What she'd meant to him was another matter altogether.

It had been a tempestuous relationship. Or as tempestuous as it could get with a middle-aged homicide sergeant who kept getting distracted by minor annoyances like crime. For one thing, Cora lived in Bakerhaven and Crowley lived in New York. Cora could drive in and see him every night, which, pleasant though that might be, did put her in a somewhat subservient position, not Cora's usual posture. She considered ousting the people subletting her apartment and moving back to the City, but that meant leaving Sherry and the baby. Though the baby was hardly a baby anymore, Jennifer was getting cuter every day, and Cora didn't want to miss it.

The other option, moving in with Crowley, had not been suggested. Even with Cora dropping subtle hints in that direction, such as, "Gee, it would be easier if I lived here," Crowley was not rising to the bait, which helped put a damper on their ardor. Cora's trips to the City became less frequent until they decided a long-distance relationship was just too stressful to maintain. It finally evolved into the "If you're here in town give me a call, but don't come all the way to see me" it was now.

Should she have called him in the intervening months? They'd agreed not to. They'd agreed to see each other when they were in town. And then the days had become weeks, weeks had become months, and the longer it was the harder it was to make the call. The call that had to be made from Manhattan couldn't be made from Bakerhaven. She had no reason to go to Manhattan, except for him. The very thing they'd agreed they would not do. Drive that distance just to see each other. A necessary agreement so as not to feel guilty when they didn't.

Whose idea had that been?

Had Crowley brushed her off?

Had Crowley moved on?

Was there someone else?

Should Cora be staking out the police station instead of the husband's office?

Was she making it up? Was she thinking too hard? She'd just called a busy cop at work to tell him she was in town and didn't have time to see him.

No. That's not what she'd said. That was his idea. She'd only told him she didn't know when she'd get off work. He could have said, "Call me when you do." But he hadn't. He'd been totally unwelcoming.

No, that wasn't fair. He said do you have time to see me. But this afternoon. In the office. Before getting on the job. Not for a romantic interlude after.

Cora stomped back to her car, certain that despite her best efforts to adhere to the letter of the law, some avenging fury would have affixed a parking ticket to her windshield, courtesy of some concealed, camouflaged, or contradictory parking sign that in some way negated it being a legal space.

There wasn't one. Cora was disappointed. She'd have loved something to be mad at besides Crowley.

What a total schmuck. Cora shook her head angrily. Well, what did she expect? Damn it to hell. She knew what men were. Why was she surprised?

Snap out of it. She had a job to do. Catching Brittany's two-timing husband with that cheap little tramp. Assuming that was what he was up to.

Of course he was. How could he possibly be doing anything different?

Cora snorted. "Men!"

Cora staked out Hank Wells' office building at 4:30, figuring it would be just like the philandering son of a bitch to get off early. Brittany's husband worked on Sixth Avenue and 50th Street, which created a bit of a problem. Meter maids of all sexes kept suggesting that Cora move her car. The ensuing discussions were counterproductive at best. The fact Cora was not arrested and booked was a minor miracle. Three times she was forced to drive off. One time she got away with driving from one side of the street to the other, but twice she was forced to circle the block, opening up the possibility that her quarry had escaped while she'd done so.

Cora was pissed. She couldn't recall TV detectives having problems with meter maids. After the second time around the block she decided to hell with it, Becky had a client, and the next meter maid who asked her to move she'd just say no and let Blondie pay the ticket. It occurred to her the meter maid wouldn't take no for an answer. What would happen then? Would it be the first time a meter maid ever called for backup? It was almost worth finding out. Cora found herself looking around, hoping for a meter maid.

Instead, Hank Wells came out the front door, large as life. Cora recognized him from the photo his loving wife had thought to bring to Becky's office. Brittany hadn't thought to bring the life insurance policy, which might have seemed relevant to the situation, since a lawyer could immediately tell if it was indeed the deadly double-jackpot policy worth killing for. But from her assessment of Becky's client, Cora was surprised the woman had even *found* Becky's office.

Hank looked just like his photograph, which figured, since it was a photo of him. He was trim and good-looking in a suit and tie, clean shaven, with wavy dark hair and flashing blue eyes. He was young, too young for her. Cora winced at the thought. Twenty in her mind's eye, Cora had often dated younger men. Not that she had any thoughts of becoming the home-wrecking hussy Becky's client had hired her to find; still the idea of washing him out as too young was unsettling at best. She wondered if it had anything to do with striking out with Crowley.

Because that's how she saw it. She'd made an overture toward the man and been rebuffed. Was this the cause of the subsequent blue funk?

Hank Wells was coming right at her. Sixth Avenue being an uptown street, she'd parked just downtown from the building so she could see him when he came out. Unfortunately, he was walking downtown, which left her no way to follow in the car. As he went by, Cora slipped out of the front seat and slammed the door. Take that, meter maid. You may ticket me, but I won't be there to move.

It was rush hour, and the avenue was filled with people getting off from work. Cora had no problem blending in with the crowd. Hank walked two blocks south and went into a Duane Reade. Cora resented it. In Manhattan there were Duane Reades every two blocks. Why couldn't the guy have gone uptown and let her keep her car?

The drugstore had only one entrance, so Cora didn't follow him in, just hung out on the corner and waited for him to reappear.

He was out five minutes later. His hands were empty. Evidently, he had bought something small. Most likely condoms, Cora figured.

Hank could have been helpful and walked back toward her car, but he didn't. Instead he stepped out in the street and hailed a cab. That he got one in rush-hour traffic was a minor miracle, but he did.

Cora glanced around helplessly. There were lots of cabs coming up Sixth Avenue, but all were occupied. There was no cab with its lights on.

Halfway down the block a cab pulled up to the curb to discharge a passenger. Cora sprinted for it, brushing aside a gentleman with a briefcase who clearly had the same idea. She reached the cab, practically ripped the passenger who was attempting to pay out the back door, and hopped in.

"Follow that cab!" she said. She felt like she was in a forties noir movie. The TV monitor with a clip from the Jimmy Kimmel show broke the spell.

So did the turbaned driver, who turned around to ask, "Which cab?"

The man had a point. Hired cabs were passing them even as he spoke.

"Pass as many as you can," Cora said. "I'll tell you when I see him."

The guy might not have looked like a NASCAR driver, but he drove like one. In four blocks Cora spotted the cab with Hank in it.

"That's him. Drop back, but don't lose him. Go where he goes."

Hank's cab went up Sixth to 59th Street, hung a left to Columbus Circle, continued uptown on Broadway, and pulled up on the corner of 84th.

Cora stopped her cab halfway down the block. She paid the meter, cursing the charge, and hopped out.

Hank was already walking east on 84th. Cora hurried to the corner, praying she hadn't lost him in the few seconds he'd been out of sight. Not to worry. He was on the sidewalk, stepping right along.

Cora's pulse quickened. It was a residential neighborhood on the Upper West Side. Fertile ground for a love nest. This could be pay dirt.

Or not.

Halfway down the block Hank fished his wallet out of his back pocket, pulled out a cardboard ticket stub, and walked into a parking garage.

Cora watched him drive off. She didn't try to follow. Hank was most likely going home, and the idea of taking a metered cab to Bakerhaven was more than she could bear. Most cabbies would probably refuse anyway. The day was a washout. There was nothing to but go back downtown and see how many tickets were on her car.

None.

Her car had been towed.

Brittany Wells was even younger than Cora had expected, and her expectations had been low. She was also furious, which, coupled with her age, gave the impression she was having a temper tantrum.

"You lost him?" Brittany said. She looked like someone had stolen her Barbie doll. "I didn't want you to lose him."

Cora bit her lip. Several responses flew to mind, such as, "Duh," "Gee, I thought that's what I was supposed to do," or, "Thank you for telling me; now that I know I'll do better."

Before she could blurt out something withering, Becky jumped in. "Be reasonable. When your husband took a cab uptown, there was no way to know he was going for his car."

"Why not? That's where he parked it."

"As it turned out. But there was no way to anticipate that."

"But that's where he always parks it."

Cora was sufficiently stunned by that remark that Becky was able to intervene before her detective ripped her client limb from limb.

"Excellent. If he always parks there, we can prepare for it. Cora, can you get a parking spot behind him on the same block?"

"Not on the street. I can get a garage closer to Broadway."

"Would that work?"

"Sure. I'll get my car first, be waiting when he comes out with his." Cora shrugged. "Not that it will do any good."

Brittany looked at her sharply. "What do you mean by that?"

"What time did your husband get home last night?"

"What's that got to do with it?"

"Humor me. What time was it?"

"He got home around seven."

"There you are. What with rush-hour traffic and stopping at the drugstore, seven o'clock isn't late. It certainly didn't leave time for a romantic interlude. From this we can conclude if your husband's fooling around, he's doing it in the City. Once he gets his car, he goes home."

"Just because he did it once—"

Cora put up her hand. "Sure, sure. I could be wrong. I believe my ex-husband Melvin could point to an occasion. He tried hard enough during the divorce proceedings. Now that I know, I will take the precaution of parking on the block where Hubby parks. But for my money, his sweetie's in New York."

"You think he has one?"

"*If* he has one," Becky said.

"So, you bring the policy?" Cora said.

Brittany frowned. "Huh?"

"The insurance policy," Becky said. "Cora, that's my concern, not yours."

"So concern yourself with it. What's it say? Is there any point in going through this whole charade?"

"Charade?" Brittany said. "What do you mean, 'charade'?"

"Oh," Cora said. "Well, it's a party game where I act something out and you try to guess what it is."

Becky shot Cora a warning glance. "It's not a charade. It's

precautionary surveillance. We hope it doesn't mean anything, but if it does, we want to be prepared. So, let's take a look at the policy and see if it really is worded the way you think. If it's not, you've got nothing to worry about."

"Oh, yeah? What if it's not but my husband thinks it is?"

Cora shot Becky a look. That remark was sharper than either of them would have given Brittany credit for. Maybe she wasn't so dumb.

"Good point," Becky said. "But let's take a look and see what the facts really are before we start speculating on how someone may have misinterpreted them."

Brittany blinked twice. "Huh?"

On the other hand, maybe she was that dumb, Cora thought wryly. "The insurance policy. Let your lawyer take a gander at the double-indemnity clause."

"Oh. I don't have it."

"Why not?"

"I can't find it. I looked all over."

"Your husband hid the insurance policy?"

"Oh, I don't think he'd do that," Brittany said. "I think he just put it away and I don't know where."

"So ask him where it is."

"I can't do that."

"Why not?"

"He'd want to know why I wanted to know. I can't tell him my lawyer's trying to find out if he wants to kill me."

"Does he know you hired a lawyer?"

"Of course not."

"Tell him you want to look it over and see if you understand it."

"Why?"

"So you can find out where he keeps it."

Brittany gave Cora a look as if *she* were the moron. "No, what do I tell *him* when he asks me why I want to read it?"

Becky put up her hand to cut off Cora's response. "I think we're getting sidetracked here, Brittany. I need to see the policy. I don't care how you get it, or what you tell your husband. I just want to see it."

Brittany looked dubious. "Well, all right. I'll try to bring it in tomorrow." She got up to go.

"In that case," Becky said, "do you want us to hold off on the surveillance?"

Brittany turned back in the doorway. "Huh?"

"Do you want to hold off until I look at the policy before we tail your husband? He didn't go anywhere yesterday, and it may be there's no need."

Brittany shook her head. "He's up to something. I'm sure of it." She looked at Cora. "Don't lose him this time and maybe you'll find out."

Cora watched her leave, turned to Becky. "She paid you yet?"

"Not nearly enough. Of course, I didn't know there'd be a two-hundred-and-fifty-five-dollar towing charge on the expense account."

"Does *she* know it yet?"

"I thought it would be more tactful to bring it up on a day you *hadn't* lost her husband."

"I laid that money out of pocket."

"You afraid you won't be reimbursed?"

"I know I will. I'd like the money to come out of her pocket, not yours."

"The point is we're still on the case. Now you know where to park you can give her husband a run for his money."

"Right. I can rack up some mileage following him home."

Becky cocked her head. "Didn't go well with Crowley?"

"How do you know that?"

"Are you kidding? The woman wants to send you back to the City, you're trying to talk your way out of it. If he were waiting for you, we wouldn't be having this conversation; you'd already be gone."

Cora started to flare up, sighed. "Yeah, it didn't go well. I had to work and he had to work."

"You had to work before and it never stopped you. Of course, you had the advantage of getting arrested."

"You think I should commit some crime to attract his attention?"

"I wouldn't put it past you. So, what's the real problem?"

Cora scowled. "*That's* the real problem. I get to the City, Crowley's at work. I stake out an office building, tail this numbnuts around till he gets in his car, and follow him back to Bakerhaven. Wonderful. We accomplish no useful purpose except getting me the hell out of New York. If on the other hand, the guy is fooling around, I get to hang out and watch him do it."

"That's not exactly in the job description."

"It would be if I could swing it. And I still gotta follow him home, don't I?"

"I suppose so."

"So," Cora said. "You'll pardon me if I seem somewhat negative, but just between you and me, what's the upside?"

"Are you kidding?" Becky smiled. "I got a retainer."

There was no reason to call Crowley again, so Cora did. "Hey, big boy, how's police biz?"

"Cora. This is getting to be a habit."

"Yeah. I keep staking guys out and you keep having police work."

"You kill him and I'll come arrest you."

"That's practically what Becky said."

"How is your lawyer?"

"Employed. That's why I'm here. To see if anyone's having sex in New York City."

There was a slight pause before Crowley said, "What's the verdict?"

"Nothing so far. I'm ever hopeful."

"What's your plan?"

"I don't have a plan. Just marching orders. Stake out the son of a bitch and see where he goes."

"Sounds like typical PI work."

"You ever do it?"

"You kidding me? I'm a sergeant. I got detectives to do it."

"Got one I could use for this?"

"Sorry. That's the type of scandal would get me suspended."

"Well, we wouldn't want any scandal, would we?"

Another short pause before, "Good luck with your stakeout."

"No such thing," Cora said. "If I don't find anything, I failed. If I find it, I'm out of a job."

Crowley chuckled. "You have a way with words." He was one of the few people who knew Cora was an out-and-out fraud. "As long as they don't involve a puzzle."

"Well, good to talk to you," Cora said. "Maybe one of these days we'll hook up."

"That would be nice. You get off early, give me a call," Crowley said, and hung up.

Cora drove up Sixth Avenue in a much better mood. That was a vast improvement on yesterday's phone call. She wasn't getting to see him, but he'd sounded friendly, welcoming. Yesterday he'd sounded hassled. Yeah, a big improvement.

Maybe she'd have better luck with Brittany's hubby, too.

Hank Wells came out of his office building with a lilt in his step, which was not exactly how Cora would have described it. For her money, he looked like a guy who hoped to get lucky.

So did she.

Cora wondered if he'd head for the drugstore again. He didn't. He stepped out in the street to hail a cab.

Cora smiled. For once the gods were with her. There was no way he was getting a cab first. The cab would have to go by her to pick him up.

Sure enough, Cora nailed the first cab up Sixth Avenue. The driver had a thick accent and no vowels in his name. He turned around and grunted something, most likely, "Where to?"

Cora pointed. "See that man trying to hail a cab?"

The driver pointed, said something indistinguishable.

"That's right," Cora said.

The driver kicked the cab in gear, started straight toward Hank.

"Stop!" Cora screamed.

The startled driver slammed on the brakes, skidded toward the curb, and nearly knocked a bike messenger into a baby carriage. He pulled the cab to a stop and turned around in his seat to see why his passenger had suddenly lost her mind.

The outraged cry caught in his throat. His eyes widened. He pointed his finger at her. "Puzzle Lady! You Puzzle Lady!" His face broke into an idiotic grin.

Cora couldn't believe it. A fan.

"That's right. And I'm on the job. I'm supposed to follow that guy and see where he goes. Can you help me do that?"

Cora was a little concerned about how that might translate, but she needn't have worried. The cabbie nodded enthusiastically and turned to size up his quarry, who had just flagged down a second cab.

The cabbie had no problem tagging along, though he drove Cora crazy constantly turning around to grin at her while piloting the cab up Sixth Avenue with one hand. When he ran the light at 56th Street after losing half a block with his no-look driving, Cora couldn't wait for the guy to drop her safely at the garage.

She never got the chance. At the corner of 83rd Street Hank's cab swung a left off Broadway, crossed West End Avenue, and headed for Riverside Drive. Halfway down the block the cab stopped and Hank got out.

"Pull up here," Cora said.

Her cabbie looked betrayed. They were about fifty yards behind, his quarry was leaving, and she was dismissing his services. Well, what did he expect her to do? Invite him to leave his cab and tag along?

There was twelve bucks on the meter. Cora gave the cabbie fifteen and got out.

He didn't drive off. Cora snorted in exasperation. She didn't have time to deal with him. Hank was going somewhere and she had to follow. A nosy cabbie was the last thing she needed.

Cora walked casually down the block keeping Hank in sight. It was a slightly iffy proposition. If he saw her, he'd recognize her. Bakerhaven was a small town. He'd have seen her somewhere or know her from TV. But the odds of him turning in her direction were slim.

He'd told the cabbie where to stop. Where he was going would be right there.

It was. Hank went across the street and up the steps of a brownstone. There was a row of buttons next to the door. He pushed one, was buzzed inside.

In this instance, Cora had to admit, she was lucky it was winter. It was dark out and there were lights in the windows. At least in two of the apartments, on the second and third floors. The first and fourth floors were dark.

Cora wondered if they were floor-though apartments or if the floors were divided up. She wasn't close enough to see the buttons. How many were there? Should she cross and take a look?

Not yet. She held her place, watched the windows from across the street. Out of the corner of her eye she could see the cabbie, inching up the street. She thrust out her hand, palm up. The cabbie stopped. Cora didn't look at him, continued watching the building, praying for a miracle.

Her prayers were answered. A face appeared in the third-floor window. It was Hank. A moment later, a slender woman's arm reached up and pulled the shade.

Jackpot! Brittany Wells was right. Hubby did have a sweetie on the side; he was hanging out with her whenever he could. That's why he had a garage in the neighborhood. It wasn't just that it was cheaper than a midtown garage. It was where he needed his car.

The importance of Becky Baldwin checking out the double-indemnity clause had suddenly multiplied.

Cora wondered if she should report in. It seemed like a bad idea. For one thing, she didn't have a cell phone. For another, she had queasy visions of *New York Post* headlines like LOVE NEST BLOODBATH. Much as Becky needed the work, defending Brittany Wells from a multiple-homicide rap probably wasn't what she had in mind. Particularly with a guilty client. What was she going to do, plead the unwritten law?

Besides, Cora didn't even know who the woman was. Any disclosure at this point would be premature.

There was nothing to stop Cora from crossing the street and looking at the doorbells.

Except the nosy cabbie.

Cora went back, walked up to the driver's side window. He rolled it down.

"Show's over. I don't need you anymore."

The cabbie acted like he didn't comprehend. "Wait?" he ventured hopefully.

Cora shook her head. "Go," she said firmly, and pointed down the street.

Reluctantly, the cabbie drove off.

Cora crossed the street, went up the front steps of the brownstone, looked at the bells. There were indeed two buzzers per floor, marked F and R. 3F, presumably third-floor front, was marked M. Greer. Cora dug in her purse, fished out a notebook and pen, copied it down.

Cora shoved the notebook back in her purse and went to stake out the apartment from across the street. She had just found a nice place in the shadows behind an SUV when she noticed a taxi that looked familiar parked by a fireplug at the corner of Riverside Drive. She walked down the street to check it out. Sure enough, it was the same cab. She knocked on the driver's window, gave him her best you-don't-want-to-mess-with-me stare, and jerked her thumb.

Third time's the charm. When the light changed, the cabbie turned right and drove up Riverside Drive. Cora figured he was actually gone.

Cora hurried back, set up surveillance on apartment 3F. Hoped like hell her quarry hadn't escaped while she was dismissing the cab. But that wasn't likely. There was no way the guy was in and out that quickly unless he was buying drugs.

There was a new thought and one Brittany hadn't even suggested. Could the guy be a dope fiend without his wife even knowing? Well, he could, but in that case he was buying from a shapely young thing with her own apartment. No, every instinct told Cora the situation was exactly as it seemed. In which case, he'd be upstairs for a while.

It was close to forty-five minutes. Long enough for all practical purposes. Cora had no doubt the young gentleman had availed himself of the opportunity. In which case he'd be going home, so as not to alert his slow but not-quite-brain-dead wife to his perfidy. Most likely, he'd be heading for his car.

He was. Cora tailed him to the garage. They passed hers on the way, and Cora could have gotten her car, except she saw no need. Hubby would be on his way to Bakerhaven. Anyway, he wasn't the objective anymore.

Cora went back, sized up the building. She had to figure out who the woman was. She could ring the buzzer, talk to her over the intercom, try to finesse her into saying her name. Or she could finagle her way through the downstairs door, either by ringing apartments at random until someone buzzed her in, picking the downstairs lock, or waiting for someone to go in or out and timing her approach so as to catch the door before it had an opportunity to close. Then she could go up to the third floor, bang on the door of 3F. Even if the woman wouldn't let her in, just opened the door on a safety chain, she'd get a look at her through the crack in the door. The downside was the woman would get a look at *her*. And if vowelless cabbie knew her from TV, what chance would she stand against a slinky femme fatale? If the bimbo recognized her and told Hubby, the jig would be up.

Of course, that was just the ditzy client's assessment of the situation. What the actual situation was, was anybody's guess. But that didn't matter. Brittany was the client, and going against her wishes was not going to win anyone any gold stars.

All right. Cora had an address, an apartment number, a last name, and a first initial. Assuming that information was correct, how would a private investigator go about verifying who the woman actually was? More to the point, how could she check her out without letting her know she was being checked out?

Cora had no idea.

Then it occurred to her she knew a cop.

Sergeant Crowley had put on weight. The stomach Cora was lying across seemed somewhat firmer than it had before. The two-day stubble was the same, however. So was his lazy smile. It was a nice smile, made up for so many other lapses. The man's good humor was one of the things that had attracted Cora to him in the first place. As she snuggled on his chest, she couldn't help thinking it was what she missed the most.

Not that he was not a perfectly satisfactory lover. But as Cora had been married some five or six times, men held few surprises. She was pleased by their passion, but it was not their only allure.

Crowley had gotten to her. Putting the relationship on hiatus had been tough, though she had quite understood the situation. But it was great to be back in the Greenwich Village apartment with the cop with the poster of Jimi Hendrix on the wall.

Cora smiled as she traced patterns on his chest. "Gee, all I said was could you check out an address for me. You are one fast worker."

"Well, we never stood on ceremony much," Crowley said.

"That's for sure. On the other hand, it's been a while."

"Eighty-seven days, but who's counting."

"Eighty-seven days?" Cora said.

"I made it up. Was I close?'

"I wasn't counting."

"Of course not."

"What you been up to lately?"

"Same old same old. Catching crooks, mainly. How about you?"

"Oh, business as usual."

"That must be time-consuming. Pretending to write crossword puzzles."

"I construct sudoku."

"I stand corrected. Only half your life's a fraud."

"Just because I don't construct puzzles doesn't mean I'm not the Puzzle Lady. I also film TV commercials."

"So you want me to ID this woman?"

"Yes, I do. All your attempts to distract me notwithstanding."

"And how am I supposed to do this?"

"Well, you could bang on her door, drag her down to the police station."

"False arrest. You want me to commit false arrest?"

"I was afraid you wouldn't go for that. How about selling tickets to the policeman's ball?"

"I can't drag her downtown for that."

"You don't have to drag her downtown, just get her to open her door."

"You want me to sneak you into her building, hide you in the stairwell, and then attempt to fraudulently solicit money for a non-existent charity?"

"Would that be a problem?"

"No, it sounds like fun. If you're a college student. I'm a New York City homicide officer. I cannot abuse my position to satisfy the whims of a private citizen."

"Wuss."

"Hey, I'm a pro. I got principles." Crowley reached for the phone. "You ordering food? We didn't decide on Thai or Indian."

"Yeah." Crowley spoke into the phone. "Hey, Perkins. Six-twenty-four West Eighty-third Street. Apartment Three F. Who lives there?"

Brittany was crushed. "So he is having an affair."

"So it would seem."

"But you don't know for sure."

"Well, I didn't actually see them in bed together," Cora said.

"Don't be stupid," Brittany said.

It was all Cora could do to hold her tongue. She could feel her teeth grinding. The amused glance Becky was giving her didn't help. "No, I don't know for sure that he's having an affair. I saw him go to her apartment. I saw her pull down the shades."

"But you don't know what she looks like."

Actually, Cora did. Perkins had managed to get Crowley a copy of her driver's license photo from the DMV. Surely a misdemeanor, if not a criminally indictable offense. When you got a cop breaking rules, Cora figured, it was kind of hard to get him to stop.

"Would you like me to stake her apartment with a camera?" Cora said.

"I'd like you to do something. I have to know if my husband is having an affair."

"Well, you have to admit we've made some progress in that direction," Becky said, forestalling Cora's angry retort. "Yesterday you didn't know if your husband was seeing anyone. Now you know he is. You may not know why, at least you may not be sure, but you certainly have reason to suspect. So, it would seem there was some foundation to your initial apprehension."

"Huh?" Brittany said.

"Oh, for God's sake," Cora said. "You thought your husband might be trying to kill you because he was having an affair. It appears that might be true."

"Exactly," Becky said. "So let's have a look at the insurance policy."

Brittany shrugged. "I don't have it."

"She *told* you to get it," Cora said accusingly.

Brittany's eyes flashed. "Excuse me. Who's hiring who?"

"You're hiring me," Becky said. "And I'm hiring her. And we're all working together toward the same end. In light of what Cora told me, I need to see that policy. Now, how can we make that happen?"

"I don't know."

"If he's at work all day, why can't you search the house?" Cora said.

"I have searched the house. I can't find it."

"You want *me* to search the house?" Cora said. "I'm good at it."

"I don't think it's in the house. I think he has it at work."

"Tell him you want to see it," Cora said.

"I can't do that."

"Because then he'll know you found out he has a girlfriend and deduced he wants to kill you," Cora said sarcastically.

Brittany completely missed the irony. "Exactly. So who is she?"

"You don't want to know."

"Of course I want to know. That's what I'm paying you for."

"You're not paying me. You're paying her. And you're not paying her to find out who your husband's having an affair with; you're paying her to make sure he doesn't kill you to cash in on his insurance policy."

"I'm paying her to do what I tell her. You want me to tell her to fire you?"

Becky put up her hands. "Ladies, ladies, we are getting far afield. I let Cora sit in on this meeting because she's the one who did the legwork and I figured you'd want to get your report firsthand. If that's not a good idea, I won't have her at our next meeting. But I'm not firing her on your say-so. You're retaining me as an attorney to protect your interests. As your attorney, I'm advising you what your interests are. If it's in your best interests to have her in my employ, that's what I'm going to do. If you don't choose to follow my advice, you are certainly free to hire another attorney."

"You're the only one in town!" Brittany cried in exasperation.

Becky smiled. "Yes. That is one of the few advantages of practicing law in Bakerhaven. Now then, we found out your husband is seeing another woman, and you'd like to know who she is. Certainly a reasonable request. Though I'm sure Cora could give you a dozen reasons why it's not a good idea."

"I don't understand."

"What a surprise," Cora said. Before Brittany could react, she went on. "If Becky wants you to know who she is, I'll tell you who she is. Even though it would be better if you didn't."

"Why?"

"Say the woman's found dead. The police look for someone with a motive. How about the jealous wife whose husband was cheating on her? Jackpot! Warm up the cell. I wish all cases were this easy."

"She's not going to turn up dead."

"No? Even if you go see her? Argue with her? Accuse her of stealing your husband? A catfight escalates into violence. You struggle; she falls; she hits her head. 'Uh-oh. Should I call the cops? It's an accident. At worst, self-defense. But what if they think it's a murder? Maybe I should cover my tracks, get out of here. Wipe the apartment down for fingerprints, sneak out, pretend I was never there.'"

"That's ridiculous."

"It certainly is. They always catch you when you do that. Sometimes it's not even your fault. The cops find a message from her on your husband's answering machine. They figure you heard it. It doesn't matter if you did or not; they fry you for it."

Brittany frowned.

"And that's just the accident. Your husband can put two and two together, figure out what you've done. If he's a vindictive son of a bitch—and most husbands are—he's going to lead the cops in your direction. Hell, he'll practically have to. Because otherwise they'll pick on him. Figure she was his problem, insisting he leave his wife. And he doesn't want to bust up his marriage, so he kills her to shut her up."

"Can you shut *her* up?" Brittany said.

"Cool it, Cora. You're freaking my client out."

"Not my intention. I was just pointing out why sharing the information I gathered might not be a hot idea. But it's not up to me. I work for you. You have my report. You want to show it to her, that's your business."

Brittany stuck out her hand. "Gimme."

Becky picked up the paper with the woman's name and address and passed it over.

Brittany read the name. "'Madeline Greer.'"

"Right," Cora said. "Probably calls herself Maddy. So now you got the name and address. What you gonna do? You gonna call on this woman?"

"No."

"Confront your husband with her?"

"Certainly not."

"So," Becky said, "without the document, that's all I can do. You get ahold of it, bring it in. Or if your husband says anything that sheds any light on the situation, let me know."

"In the meantime you might want to avoid moonlit drives on wooded lanes," Cora said. "If you go out alone, check your brakes before driving over any mountain roads. I also wouldn't eat anything he won't."

Brittany's mouth fell open. "That's awful."

"Yeah, it is. Particularly if you're fond of spicy foods. They're good at hiding poison."

Brittany put up her hands. "Okay, okay, I get the point. You gotta find out if he's up to something. You just can't let him know you're doing it."

Brittany jammed the name and address into her purse.

"I wouldn't let your husband find that," Cora said.

"Oh, what a clever suggestion. I never would have thought of it." Brittany glared at Cora and flounced out the door.

"Well, I guess we're not fired," Cora said.

"No, but you certainly tried hard enough."

"Damn right I did. That girl spells trouble."

"You don't think she'd kill her rival?"

"I don't know what she'd do. She has a pathological fear of her husband. Which isn't always a bad thing, husbands being what they are. But in her case, there's no telling what it might drive her to. I wouldn't put it past her to kill this woman just so she wouldn't have to ask him about his insurance."

"You really don't trust her."

"Do you? I notice you didn't give her the picture."

"Okay, you got me. If she really is as neurotic as she seems, why make it easy for her? If she wants to confront this woman, she'll have to ID her first."

"Do *you* want to confront this woman?"

"That would be contrary to my client's wishes."

"*Everything* is contrary to your client's wishes. If she wants to find out if her husband's having an affair, she's certainly not making it easy." Cora frowned. "There's a thought."

"What?" Becky said.

"If she wants to find out if her husband's having an affair. Maybe she *doesn't* want to find out if her husband's having an affair."

"Then why would she hire us?"

"Why indeed?"

"Well," Becky said, "let's assume she hired us for a purpose, and go about doing it."

"Okay." Cora got up. "Looks like I'm heading back to New York."

Crowley's office was just as Cora had remembered it. Bare walls, cluttered desk, no place to sit unless you were a perp. Cora had been a perp the first time she was there, so she knew the routine. She sat on the metal folding chair, tried to look innocent. It had been easier when she was actually guilty.

Crowley shook his head. "I don't believe it. You come by my office, in the middle of the day, during work hours, you sit right there, and you ask me to violate every statute in the penal code."

"I didn't ask you to kill her."

"I count myself lucky. Look, IDing the woman was one thing. But this is not the way it works. You get me to violate some small law, then use it as a wedge to get me violate more and more, and the next thing you know I'm suspended from duty pending an internal affairs investigation."

"I'm not asking you to do anything illegal."

"Blackmail's illegal."

"Who said anything about blackmail?"

"You did."

"I'm a private citizen. They can't prosecute you for something I said."

"It's not what you said. It's what you want me to do."

"Did I ask you to blackmail anybody? Not at all. I asked you to *pretend* to blackmail someone. The type of thing that cops do all the time. A police scam. An undercover operation. Like a buy-and-bust."

"This isn't a buy-and-bust."

"It could be. Plant some drugs on her, arrest her, see if her boyfriend bails her out."

"That is a *really* low-percentage plan."

"Yeah. Wanna do it?"

"No. Nor do I want to take part in any of the other harebrained schemes you've outlined. I happen to have a heavy caseload this afternoon. I'm glad to see you and all that, but I really gotta get back to work."

"What time you get off tonight?" Cora was trying not to sound needy, wasn't sure she quite made it.

"I don't know, but it doesn't look good. I played hooky yesterday; I'm making up for it today."

"Right," Cora said. "Two days in a row would seem like a commitment."

"Hey. Just because I won't break the law doesn't mean I'm not a nice guy."

"I know." Cora cocked her head. "Will it get you in trouble if that woman turns up dead?"

"It will if your client did it."

"She's not my client. She's Becky's."

"That's not the point. Just leave the woman alone. If I find out you tried to blackmail her, I will not be happy."

"Hey. I'm a celebrity. People know who I am. You think I can walk up to someone and try to blackmail them?"

"I have no idea what you might do."

"Not in this case. Trust me. I won't go near the woman."

Madeline Greer frowned. Her doorbell was ringing. Her doorbell shouldn't be ringing. The buzzer from downstairs should be
buzzing. If someone rang the doorbell without buzzing, they were
either someone from the building or someone with no right to be
there. Madeline didn't know anyone from the building. At least not
to socialize with, and she wasn't the type to borrow a cup of sugar
from. The super never buzzed; hell, she couldn't *find* the super unless the building was falling down. Even when a water leak on the
fourth floor sent cascades of plaster into her bathroom, she couldn't
get his attention. And no, he wasn't on the fourth floor dealing with
the leak; he was down in the basement sleeping on the cot behind
the boiler. At least according to the tenant whose plaster was in her
bathtub.

A ringing doorbell was a rarity indeed. Madeline peered out the
keyhole.

A man in a suit and tie stood in the hallway. He carried a briefcase. He had a pleasant enough face, but his hair seemed too dark
and his skin too smooth for a man his age. A funny thought, since

those two things were clearly to obscure his age. But Madeline got the impression the man was not as young as he looked.

He certainly seemed affable enough, though. The type of man instantly attractive to women. Madeline wasn't necessarily buying, but she wasn't bolting the door and calling the police, either.

She opened the door on a safety chain. "Yes?"

"Miss Greer? Miss Madeline Greer?"

"Yes."

"I'm Martin Kendrick, of Kendrick and Blake. I believe I have news for you."

"Oh?"

"Are you familiar with a man named Gerald Waldman?"

"Not that I know of."

The man nodded and smiled. "I'm glad to hear it. If he was a close friend, this would be a less pleasant occasion."

"I don't understand."

"Well, since you don't know Mr. Waldman, it won't be a shock to learn that he is dead."

"Dead?"

"Actually three months now. It's taken that long to get around to probating the will. Whether you know him or not, it would appear you are one of Mr. Waldman's beneficiaries. Of a rather substantial amount. Assuming you can prove you are the woman in question."

"Prove? What do you mean, 'prove'?"

"Well, since you don't know the man, there is some reason for doubt. Can you prove that you're actually Madeline Greer?"

"Yes, of course."

"I'm going to need see some ID—driver's license, birth certificate, passport, Social Security card—before turning over a check. And you'll have to fill out the necessary paperwork."

"What paperwork?"

He tapped the briefcase. "I have it here. It's a bit of a pain, but I can help you fill it out."

"Yes, of course."

She took off the chain, opened the door, and let her visitor in. She led him into the kitchen, sat him at the table.

He put down his briefcase, took out some forms.

"Would you like some tea or coffee?"

He smiled. "No. This won't take long. Why don't you have a seat."

Madeline sat down, composed herself. "What do you need to know?"

"How long have you been sleeping with Hank Wells?"

Her mouth fell open. "What?"

"Hank Wells. Is he a steady boyfriend, or do you have several? Not that I blame you if you do. You're an attractive woman. I could go for you myself."

Her face hardened. "Who are you?"

"I'm the silver-tongued devil who sweet-talked his way into your apartment. Now I'm the pain in the ass you have to deal with until you find a way to get me out."

"What do you want?"

He shrugged. "What does anyone want? I want money. I want money from you, and I want money from him. I don't care how much comes from whom, just so it adds up to ten grand."

"Ten grand!"

"I'm afraid so. I have some pressing needs."

"Now, see here—"

"No, *you* see here. I don't know how well this is going to sit with the people in your circle, but I don't imagine it's going to go over well in his. You did know he was married, didn't you? I can't believe you're that naïve. The guy's gotta drive back to Connecticut every night. What's he tell you, he's superstitious, he's gotta sleep in his own bed? No, you know he's married. You just don't care. His being from out of town's probably convenient. You got a part-time man you don't have to worry about."

"How do you know all this?"

"What, like it's a secret? The guy rings your doorbell, large as life, right out there for everyone to see. Hell, it would take a blind man not to notice."

"You don't understand."

"Enlighten me."

"Hank's just a friend."

He made a sound like a game-show buzzer. "Blaaah! Wrong answer. Friends don't lie to their wives about who they're seeing after work. Nope, you're the home-wrecking mistress, and unless you'd like to be named correspondent in a messy divorce proceeding, it would behoove you to talk some sense into lover boy. It will actually be pretty enlightening. Give you a chance to see how he reacts at the prospect of losing his wife."

Madeline drew herself up. "All right. I've listened to your spiel. Now get the hell out."

He shook his head. "Clearly you've never dealt with a blackmailer before. That's exactly the wrong attitude. I certainly hope Mr. Wells is better. I imagine he will be. Businessman and all. View it as a financial transaction."

He stood up, snapped his briefcase shut.

Madeline watched in stony silence. Her lower lip trembled. It was all she could do to hold herself together as she herded him to the front door.

He turned back in the doorway, smiled. "When this is over, and lover boy dumps you, you wanna go out?"

Melvin slid into the passenger seat and grinned at Cora. "Worked like a charm."

"She fell for it?"

"How could she not? I was brilliant. Sensational. I should get an Oscar nomination. Hell, even you'd have believed I was a blackmailer."

"Think she'll call him?"

"Are you kidding? She was itching to borrow my cell phone. I tell you I was great."

"Well, modesty was never one of your stronger qualities."

"Oh, what *were* my stronger qualities?"

"I'm trying to remember one."

He put his arm around her shoulders. "I could give you a hint."

"What's the matter, Melvin, you in between adolescent bimbos?"

"No, but that's never stopped me before. Never stopped you, either, as I recall."

"I'm older but wiser, Melvin. Like in the song."

"Song?"

"Actually, it's 'sadder but wiser.' From *The Music Man*. The problem with you is been there, done that."

Melvin grinned. "Yeah, and wasn't it great?"

"I recall some fleeting moments."

"Come on. Whaddya say we get a room?"

"I'm on stakeout."

"I'm not."

"So *you* get a room."

"And you'll come by when you're done?"

"No, but I'm sure you'll find someone."

"Whatsa matter, you seeing someone?"

"As a matter of fact, I am."

"So what's he doing tonight, that you're spending it with me?"

"He had ethical concerns about blackmail. I figured you didn't."

"Good thinking. Hey, we got action."

Hank Wells strode down the block, rang the doorbell.

"That's him," Cora said.

"Sure seems in a hurry."

"Yeah, you lit a fire under him, all right."

"Want me to go back and scare him to death?"

Cora shook her head. "No need. The bimbo should do a perfectly adequate job."

"Yeah. Lovers are never shy about nagging."

"Probably not a winning point of view to hit me with."

"You told me I wasn't going to win anyway. Why should I bother tiptoeing around?"

"Why indeed."

Melvin whipped out his cell phone, punched in a number. "Hey, babe. The thing didn't take as long as I thought. Wanna meet me for dinner? . . . Your choice. Fine . . . Pick you up at eight." He flipped the phone closed.

"You really dial a number, or was that just for show?"

"Oh, like you don't have a backup plan?"

"Backup to what, Melvin? You were never my first option."

"I seem to recall you married me."

"Even then."

He grinned at her. "This is nice. Sparring with someone who can throw it back. Most women can't keep up. So. You sitting on him till he comes out?"

"I'd like to know how long he's up there."

"Why? You know what they're saying."

"I'd like to know how he feels about it."

"Can't you guess?"

"I wanna see the look on his face."

"Even if it takes all night?"

Cora looked at him. "You didn't get a date, did you? You're still trying."

"I got a date. You think I wouldn't cancel it for something better?"

"Am I supposed to feel flattered?"

"If you got a look at this one, you would."

Cora sighed. "Melvin, sometimes you say just the wrong thing."

Melvin looked at his watch. "Come on, Cora. It's early yet. The night is young. You really mind if I shake this guy down for a few grand? I got alimony to pay."

Cora grinned, shook her head. The man was incorrigible. Probably why they got along so well. When they got along. They were, for all their differences, remarkably well matched. He always knew how to amuse her, if he wanted to. Or if he hadn't done something unforgivable. Which was pretty often. Considering which, it was amazing how many times she'd forgiven him.

Melvin did have alimony to pay. It occurred to her a lot of it was hers.

"What the hell," Cora said. "Take a shot at it."

Chapter

1 8

Melvin rang the buzzer, spoke into the intercom. "It's me again. I figured you guys are probably talking about me, so you might like to have me present."

There was a pause. Melvin grinned. He could imagine the fevered discussion going on between them. Then the door buzzed open. He pushed through, went upstairs.

Hank Wells met him at the door. Hank didn't look scared, and his eyes were hard. "What do you want?"

Melvin brushed by him into the room. "I've already said what I want. The only question now is whether I'm going to get it." He waved at Madeline, who was huddled fearfully on the couch. "Hey, babe. You can relax. Now it's just me and him. Now look, Hank. Here's the thing. I happen to need ten grand. You happen to have it. Or you can get it without much trouble. You can get it, can't you?"

"I'm not giving you any money."

"That's *entirely* the wrong attitude to take. In that case I would have to go to your wife." He jerked his thumb at Madeline. "She does know you're married, doesn't she? I mean, I told her, but why should she take my word for it? Anyway, in that case I would be forced to see if your wife's divorce attorneys could reach some sort of arrangement. Granted it would be more work and not as much money as if you had simply paid me, but hey, you have to take what you can get.

"But why look on the gloomy side? Your wife may *not* divorce you. Though it may not be quite as pleasant at home."

"If you go near my wife . . ."

"You'll what? Kill me. That's kind of like the moron hiring a team of lawyers to fight a parking ticket. Come on, champ. Pay the two dollars."

"Get out."

"Well, if that's the way you want it." Melvin shrugged, started for the door.

"Stop!" Hank said.

Melvin turned back. "Yeah?"

"Stay away from my wife."

"Give me a reason."

"You know the reason. If you don't, you get nothing."

"So? You're telling me I get nothing if I dont."

"If you talk to her you've burned your bridges. You've ruled out any future negotiation."

"Ah," Melvin said. "I *like* future negotiations. They imply there is something to negotiate. And I like a bone of contention. So. Here's the deal. I will give you forty-eight hours to come up with ten grand. Right here. In this apartment. Ready to deliver to me. At that time you can either give me the money or try to negotiate your way *out* of giving it to me. And that is a negotiation I would like to see.

"So. I'm sorry to intrude. The two of you have a lovely evening. See you soon."

Whistling, Melvin ducked out the door.

Brittany was beside herself. "My God, what did you do?"

"Relax," Becky said. "Everything is fine."

"Everything is *not* fine. Hank came back last night and I could hardly believe it."

"Hardly believe what?"

"The mood he was in. I've never seen him like that."

"Like what?"

"For one thing, he was drunk."

"He doesn't get drunk that often?"

"He doesn't drink. Except last night. He was lurching around, slurring his words."

"That would be a good time to ask him about the insurance policy," Cora said.

Becky shot her a dirty look. "And what did he say?"

"He said he had a hard day at work."

"Did you tell him he was drunk?" Cora asked.

Brittany looked horrified. "No, I hoped he wouldn't notice."

"You hoped he wouldn't notice he was drunk?"

"No, that I knew it. I was afraid he'd think I was looking at him funny."

"So he told you he had a hard day at work," Becky prompted, trying to redirect the conversation.

"Yes. And he *didn't* have a hard day at work. He left work early."

"How do you know?"

"Because someone from the office called to see if he was home yet. But he wasn't. He must have been with her." She looked at Cora. "Was he? You were watching, weren't you? Was he with her?"

Cora looked at Becky.

Becky said, "Here is where we want to be very careful."

"Careful? Careful about what?"

"Not to make an irresponsible statement that can be taken the wrong way."

"Oh, my God, you lawyers. Hank warned me about lawyers."

"Hank warned you about her?" Cora said.

"No, not her. Just lawyers. Any lawyers. He said we didn't need them messing in our business."

"What was this in regard to?" Becky said.

"It was—" Brittany broke off. "What's that got to do with it? I asked you a simple question. Did he see her or not?"

"He saw her. Whether he saw her in a romantic manner is something else."

"That's what you've gotta find out."

"How?" Cora said. "Pop out of the bedroom closet with a flash camera? I'm doing my best, but I'm rather hamstrung by the fact you're afraid to ask your husband a simple question."

"Well, what *are* you doing? Why is my husband so upset?"

"You wanna handle this?" Cora said.

"I think I better," Becky said.

Becky gave Brittany a bowdlerized version of what had happened, trying to sketch Cora in the best possible light. It wasn't easy. Halfway through, Brittany's mouth was hanging open. By the end she looked positively murderous.

"You blackmailed my husband?" she said incredulously.

"It seemed like a good idea at the time," Cora said.

"Is she insane? Do you hire crazy people? I came to you for legal advice. And what do you do? You blackmail my husband. You drive him to drink. It's a wonder he didn't kill me last night."

"Was he angry at you?" Cora said.

"He was angry at the world. I just tried to stay out of his way. This morning he didn't say a word. He came down, ate breakfast, left for work. You should have seen the look on his face. I knew something was wrong. I thought he might have spotted someone watching him. Which would have been bad enough. But this? You had a blackmailer approach him and demand money?"

"Just to see if he'd cooperate," Cora said. "It's not like we took any money from him. We just threatened him. Just to see if he'd play ball."

"And you still don't know if she's his girlfriend."

"We got a pretty good idea. He didn't tell us to go to hell. He said he'd get back to us. And he was terrified we'd tell you."

"Of course he was. He doesn't know you're involved. He thinks it's some ruthless blackmailer who's gonna spill the beans. Put me on my guard. How's he gonna kill me then?"

"How is that a bad thing?" Cora said. "Unless you want him to kill you."

"What are you, stupid? It's a bad thing if you drive him to an act of desperation. A blackmailer's gonna tell his wife. He's gotta kill her before he does."

"That doesn't make any sense."

"It makes sense to me."

"Then you're not thinking straight," Cora said. "A blackmailer's gonna tell my wife I'm having an affair. So what do I do? I kill my wife so he can't tell her? Does that solve my problem? I don't think so. The guy's blackmailing me about having an affair. You think he might blackmail me about killing my wife?"

"How would he know you did it?"

"Are you kidding me? The husband *always* did it. Don't you ever read murder mysteries?"

Brittany turned to Becky. "I can't deal with this woman. She's hung up on crime novels. My husband isn't. He thinks like a normal person. If he's planning to kill me for the insurance money, that's what he's going to do. And you've got your ace detective acting out the plot from some detective story."

"Not anymore you don't," Cora said. "I'm through. I wash my hands of this whole affair."

"Hold on," Becky said. "What is this, the third grade? I feel like the playground monitor. You two play nice or I'll send you to the principal's office? Cora, you're not quitting. Brittany, you can keep me on or not, but if you do, Cora's working for me, so I need you to get along. Now, that's the situation. What do you want us to do?"

"I don't know. I've gotta think. This is just awful." Brittany stood up. "Don't do anything until I tell you. You just make it worse." She shook her head. "I don't believe this. I thought I was hiring a lawyer."

With that, Brittany stalked out, slamming the door.

Cora turned to Becky.

"That went well."

Sherry was feeding Jennifer lunch, a risky enterprise. Jennifer was too big to sit in the high chair, too small to sit at the table. The result was a compromise where Jennifer knelt on a chair and propelled food in the vicinity of her mouth, sometimes with utensils and sometimes with her bare hands. The result was a bonanza for Buddy, who scampered back and forth under the table, cleaning the floor as fast as it was littered.

Cora prudently avoided such luncheons after a glob of sweet potato had necessitated a complete change of outfit, not to mention an unscheduled shampoo. It occurred to her with so many opportunities to enjoy her grandniece there was no reason not to opt for those that did not involve food.

"Didn't see you last night," Sherry said. "Were you busy?"

"You might say that."

"Would you care to elaborate?"

"After lunch," Cora said. "I gotta check my e-mail."

Cora went into the office and logged on to the computer. The e-mail was all spam. She made short work of it, then checked out the Facebook page that Sherry maintained for her. Cora would have liked to maintain her own Facebook page, but unfortunately the majority of posts dealt with puzzle-related matters. A few of them Cora could have actually answered, but she would have rather been hit by a Mack truck. She scanned the messages for marriage proposals, always amusing and never tempting in the least. The thought of being married to a crossword enthusiast was more than she could bear. The same grounds had scuttled the occasional tentative overtures of local cruciverbalist Harvey Beerbaum.

Cora had moved on to eBay when there came the patter of little feet and small arms wrapped themselves around her leg.

"Don't worry; her hands are clean," Sherry said, trailing along behind.

"It's her face I'm concerned with," Cora said. Jennifer's cheek was glued to her thigh.

"She's washed, dried, and ready for her close-up. Be a sport and give her a break."

"Okay, Jennifer," Cora said. She lifted her into her lap, turned her around to face the computer. "Wanna see what's new in daytime drama?"

"You are not getting her hooked on soap operas," Sherry said.

"Go ahead, kid. Push any key. Maybe Auntie Cora will get lucky."

"Where was Auntie yesterday?" Sherry said. "If you don't mind my asking."

"Oh. Well, I was gonna shack up with a police officer, but he had to work, so I called my ex-husband and blackmailed a businessman."

"What?"

Cora filled Sherry in on her recent escapades.

"Oh," Sherry said. "And how did Becky's client feel about all this?"

"She can't decide whether to thank me or fire me."

"I'd call that a mixed review."

"Actually, she wanted to fire me, but Becky wouldn't let her."

"What did she do then?"

"Said she had to think things over."

"That's understandable. I would imagine her brain was exploding."

"She's not very bright."

"Neither are you. Good lord, what were you thinking?"

The phone rang.

"You wanna get that? I got a baby on my lap."

Jennifer gave her a pout. "I'm a *big* girl!"

"Right. I have a big girl on my lap. So big I can hardly lift her. I don't know how I'll ever get her off. You're going to have to help me."

Sherry picked up the phone. "Hello? . . . Yeah, just a minute." She stuck out the receiver to Cora. "It's Becky."

Cora shifted Jennifer's weight to her left hand, scooped up the phone with her right. "Yeah, Becky. What's up?"

"Better get in here."

Brittany was practically frothing at the mouth. "I can't believe this is happening!"

"What's happening?" Cora said.

"Her husband's not at work," Becky said. Cora could tell it was taking her an effort not to roll her eyes.

"So what?"

"So what?" Brittany said. "What do you mean, 'so what'? You riled him up. You backed him into a corner. Now he's coming to kill me."

"No, he's not."

"Oh, yeah? He's not in the office. How can that be? He's always in the office. If he's not in the office it's because you put him in the position where he has to kill me."

Cora rubbed her forehead. "Give me a break. If he's not in the office, he's probably with her."

Becky gave her a why-in-the-world-would-you-say-that? look.

"Well, it's the truth, isn't it?" Cora said. "If he's having an affair, he's having an affair. If he's in trouble, he's going to go to her. I mean, this is not rocket science here."

"Is that supposed to make me happy?" Brittany said icily.

"Nothing I say is going to make you happy. I'm just trying to make some sense of the situation. The thing that makes the most sense is if he's not at work he's probably with her."

"Well, we don't know, because you're not on the job."

"You didn't *want* me on the job. You wanted to fire me, for God's sake."

Again, Becky flashed a not-exactly-the-line-of-argument-I'd-like-you-to-take look. "The point is," Becky said, "no matter how rational it may be, Brittany is under the impression her husband is coming here to kill her and she'd like us to do something about it."

"I beg your pardon?" Cora said.

"She wants to be placed in protective custody."

"By the police?"

"No, by us. Specifically, by you. You have a gun and I don't. You're the tough PI. I'm the ladylike lawyer."

"You've gotta be kidding."

"No, I'm actually rather ladylike."

"Damn it," Cora said. "Look here, you don't need protection."

"Oh, no? I just found out you gave my husband forty-eight hours to pay up. Didn't mention that little tidbit, did you? Of course not. That makes it so much worse. Now he's gotta kill me before tomorrow."

"Oh, for God's sake!"

Becky put up her hand. "Brittany feels she needs protection, at least until the deadline has passed. I pointed out since you set up the deadline, you can call it off."

"And what will my husband think then? The blackmailer had a change of heart? I never heard anything so stupid. A blackmailer made a demand. My husband has to either meet it or beg for more time."

"I would think the more-time option seemed preferable."

"Well, I'm not in a position to suggest that, am I? We don't know what my husband's going to do. If his plan was to kill me all along, why in the world wouldn't he want to do it now?"

It was all Becky could do to suppress a smile. From the look Cora had just given her, it was clear the Puzzle Lady could also see the desirability of that option.

"So," Becky said. "Whether or not you agree, Brittany is of the opinion that her husband is going to kill her between now and to-morrow afternoon. So she wants you to be her bodyguard."

"Wonderful," Cora said. "You don't think he might notice a woman with a gun sleeping between the two of you in bed?"

"Don't be silly," Brittany said. "He's not going to kill me when he's home."

Cora blinked. "What?"

"Like you said, they always suspect the husband. Is he going to kill me when the two of us are alone in the house? I don't think so. He's going to kill me when he's not around."

Cora started to make a sarcastic comment, then shrugged. "In a whacky way, that makes sense."

"He's going to kill me when he's in New York. Like now. He'll slip away from work, hope nobody notices. Only I called and asked for him, so they *did* notice. Only he doesn't know that, so he could be on his way to kill me right now."

"Not knowing you've consulted a lawyer whose ace detective is responsible for having him blackmailed."

"Exactly. See what you've done to me? Couldn't be worse if you held a gun to my head."

"And yet you still want to hire me."

"You're a dangerous woman. In a fight, I'd rather have you on my side."

"Gee, that's sweet," Cora said. "Becky, do I have to?"

"If you want to work for me, you do."

"I want to work as a detective, not a nursemaid."

"You're not a nursemaid," Brittany said. "You're a bodyguard."

"Right, right," Cora said. "You're Whitney Houston and I'm Kevin Costner. What was it? Rule one: Never let her out of your sight."

"What?" Brittany said.

Cora shook her head. "Oh, hell, Becky, she never saw *The Bodyguard*."

"I couldn't get in, either," Becky said. "It was rated R."

Cora groaned. "I forget how young you people are. Did you know there used to be a band called the Beatles?"

"Very funny," Brittany said. "I need a bodyguard. Are you going to do it or not?"

"Of course she's going to do it," Becky said. As Cora started to flare up she added, "At least she's going to listen. Tell her what you had in mind."

"Exactly what I said. I want you to stick with me until my husband gets home."

"And then I'm done?" Cora said.

"That's right."

"Whether it's six o'clock, eight o'clock, ten o'clock, whenever he gets home I'm done. You want me to stake out the house until then."

"Stake out the house? You mean like in a car, or something?"

"Well, I'm not hiding in the bushes."

"Of course not. I want you with me."

"In the house?"

"Of course."

"You want your husband to come home and find me in the house?"

"That's the whole point. You see him, and he sees you. He's not going to kill me when you're a witness that he's there. How's he going to claim he came home and found me dead?"

"She has a point," Becky said.

Cora scowled. "Just how are you going to explain the fact that I'm hanging out in your house waiting for him to get home? Just what in the world are you and I doing?"

Brittany smiled. "Solving crossword puzzles."

"Not going to happen!"

Becky put up her hand. "Cora—"

"Don't 'Cora' me! There is no way I'm teaching this woman to solve crossword puzzles. I don't care how much money she's paying."

"Why not?" Brittany said.

"You're making a misassumption. Yes, I'm the Puzzle Lady. But you're not hiring the Puzzle Lady. You're hiring Cora Felton. You want to hire a bodyguard, you'll get a bodyguard. But you're not going to get one that does tricks."

"I thought it was a good idea. I could tell him I got interested in crosswords."

"And I just volunteered to come by your house and show you how to do them? I don't think so."

Brittany crinkled up her nose. "Then why would you be there?"

Cora practically ground her teeth at the arrogance of youth. Why in the world would Brittany ever be interested in an old biddy like her? She cast a cold eye in Brittany's direction.

"Murder," Cora said.

"Huh?"

"You're interested in crime. You hear I've been involved in a few murder cases. You're thinking of writing about it."

"Writing?" Brittany made it sound like a foreign concept.

"Sorry. Lost my head. Not writing. But you're interested in it. There've been an unusually large number of murders in this town. You're curious. You've heard talk. I'm the best source of information. You're plying me with tea and scones and pumping me for information."

"Scones? I have to get scones?"

"You don't have to do anything. I'm just giving you details because you're trying to make it plausible for your husband. If we're sitting in the living room when he comes home, I won't be embarrassed answering his questions. I'm just trying to make it better for you."

"I don't know if I can get scones."

"You weren't going to feed me if we were doing crossword puzzles?"

"I hadn't thought of it."

"Yeah, well, I'm working through dinner; I'm gonna eat. And guess what? Becky's sticking you with the bill."

Brittany looked at Becky to see if that was true.

Becky nodded. "If Cora's on the job, you gotta feed her. You don't have to cook, but you do have to pay."

"Country Kitchen works for me," Cora said. "You don't have to sit with me. Hang out in the bar if you like. He's not going to kill you there."

"So you expect me to take you out to dinner? What if he gets back from work and I'm not home?"

"Excellent. He can't kill you if you aren't there."

"You're not taking this seriously."

"I am, too. I can't help it if the situation's funny."

"Let's not get off on a tangent," Becky said. "Cora's going to stick with you until your husband gets home. She's going to make sure he knows she's there. Then she's done for the night. So what happens tomorrow?"

"Hank leaves for work at eight. I'm going to leave when he does. So he can't turn around and double back. Where's a good place to go at eight o'clock?"

"Cushman's Bake Shop. You can get a scone."

Brittany gave Cora a look. "You're really hung up on scones."

"I'm on a diet and they're damn good. You wanna meet me for scones, there's nothing I can do about it. It's part of the job."

"Are you kidding?"

"Hey, you're young; you're thin; you're practically anorexic. You ever watch your weight?"

"Why?" Brittany turned to Becky. "She's not taking this seriously."

"Yes, she is. Cora, cut the crap. My client's scared and she needs reassurance. Tell her it's going to be all right."

"Oh, for goodness' sakes."

"Hey," Brittany said. "I want you there tonight when my husband gets home. Are you going to do it or not?"

Cora smiled. "Can't wait."

Hank Wells walked into his living room and stopped dead.

Cora Felton and Brittany were seated on the couch drinking tea.

"Hi, honey," Brittany said. She got up and kissed him on the cheek. "This is Cora Felton. I don't know if you've officially met. You must know who she is. She's a famous person in this town. Or anywhere else for that matter."

Hank appeared to have taken leave of his senses. He blinked twice, murmured, "You're the Puzzle Lady."

Cora put down her tea, stood with a smile. "Please. I'm just Cora Felton. And you must be Hank. Brittany has told me so much about you."

"She has?"

Cora waved her hand playfully. "Oh, nothing scandalous, I assure you. More's the pity. I could use a little excitement in my life."

Hank looked overwhelmed. Cora could understand his confusion. He's being blackmailed and he's contemplating murder. The last thing in the world he needs is to discover his wife has invited a stranger into the house.

"I was just telling Brittany about crime," Cora said. "We seem to have a great deal of it in Bakerhaven. Murder in particular. Not a great thing for the chamber of commerce, is it? Not a big selling point. 'Come to Bakerhaven; we kill off half the population.' Brittany says you weren't aware of it when you moved in."

"Weren't aware of what?" Hank said. His wits seemed to have left him.

"The crime rate, of course. Way above the norm. And it's not as if we have a big-city police force. Just a chief and two officers. Put 'em on eight-hour shifts, they'd be working seven days a week. If you want around-the-clock protection, I mean."

"I still don't understand," Hank said.

"Your wife's been hearing stories. While you're off at work. Town gossip. Of course, these things tend to be exaggerated. You don't know what's true. So she decided to go right to the source. Well, not *right* to the source. That would be Chief Harper. He's not one to talk about his exploits. Not seemly for a police chief. But I don't mind bragging a bit, if someone wants to listen. Brittany and I have been having a grand old time." Cora smiled. "But you just got home. What is it, eight fifteen? I know, I know, rush-hour traffic's a bitch. Well, let me get out of your way. It's nice to meet you and all that, but you don't need me on top of a long day. Brittany, it's been fun. Thanks for the tea. We'll pick this up again. Trust me, we've only just scratched the surface." She got to her feet. "Don't worry, I'll see myself out."

Cora stopped a moment outside the front door and assessed her performance. Not bad, she figured. The guy didn't suspect a thing. Even if he did, it was all to the good, as long as it kept him from killing his wife. All in all, it hadn't been that hard.

Of course tomorrow would be worse. Tomorrow Hank had to deal with the blackmailer. How were they going to tap-dance around that?

Cora made her way down the front path to the road. The Wellses lived in a modest two-story house on Oak Street on the outskirts of town. The driveway was just big enough for two cars, so Cora had parked in the road to leave Hank room to pull in. He'd come up the driveway and parked right next to his wife. The Wellses had his-and-her cars, a pair of identical Chevy Impalas. The license plates didn't say his and hers or any other remotely cute saying one sometimes found on vanity plates, just numbers and letters like everybody else. All in all, they were just the typical suburban couple.

Except the husband wanted to kill the wife.

If that was in fact true. From what Cora had seen, it seemed entirely more likely the whole thing was in Brittany's head.

Unless, of course, it wasn't. Short of Hubby coming up with ten thousand bucks there was really no way to tell.

On the other hand, the thought that he might kept her up well into the night. When she finally did fall asleep, it was with the nagging suspicion that along about three in the morning Chief Harper would be waking her up with a phone call to tell her Brittany was dead.

Chapter

2 4

Cora reached out, groped on the nightstand, knocked the receiver off the phone. It clattered to the floor. Cora cursed, rolled over, felt around for the phone cord. She found it, reeled it in hand over hand, plastered the receiver to her face, and said, "Hello." Realized it was upside down. Flipped it around and tried again.

A dial tone greeted her ear. Whoever they were, they'd hung up.

Except the phone was still ringing. It should have stopped when she knocked it to the floor. She hadn't noticed while she was busy retrieving the phone, but now that the task was accomplished and the dial tone encountered it was painfully obvious.

The ringing wasn't the phone; it was her new alarm clock. Cora had stopped at the mall on the way home and bought the clock to make sure she didn't oversleep. Mission accomplished. The new clock was loud enough to wake the dead. It had faithfully discharged its function. Not that Cora felt particularly grateful.

Cora stumbled out of bed, padded her way into the bathroom, turned on the shower. In her drinking days, short of more liquor, it had been the only known cure for a hangover. It didn't work, but it created the illusion one was trying. Cora stepped in, shrank back from the temperature. It was either too hot or too cold; she wasn't sure. She adjusted the water, never to her satisfaction, and managed to take a shower.

Cora got dressed, raced out to Starbucks, and bought a coffee and a scone, the latter inferior in every way to the ones Mrs. Cushman trucked in from the Silver Moon Bakery in Manhattan and passed off as her own. Cora had agreed to meet Brittany at Cushman's Bake Shop for just such a scone but had things to do first.

Her many marriages had taught her that just because a husband says he's going to do something doesn't mean he's going to do it. Her many affairs had taught her just because a wife tells you her husband's going to do something means even less. Brittany's bland assurances that her husband was going to work wouldn't have satisfied Cora even if the man hadn't been contemplating murder.

Cora drove out to Oak Street to keep an eye on Hank's house. She found a spot half-hidden by the snow-covered branches of a tree, which despite the name of the street was undoubtedly a pine. She killed the motor and the temperature immediately began to drop. She was glad for the coffee. Without it she'd have been an icicle by eight o'clock. It was still a quarter to. Cora prayed that Hank wouldn't be late. Of course, it might take a while to kill his wife.

Hank was out the door by five to eight. He hopped in his car, backed out the drive. The sun reflecting off the ice and snow made it impossible to see in the car windows. It occurred to Cora it was a good thing she'd seen him get in, or she wouldn't have known whether it was Hank or Brittany who was driving off. There was no question as to that. The only question was whether he had left his wife alive. If he hadn't, nothing Cora was about to do would matter. If he had, there were a few things she wanted to know.

Cora pulled out, followed Hank through town to the highway, where he got on, heading for New York. She followed him a couple of exits just to make sure he wasn't going to double back, before doubling back herself.

As she drove down Main Street, she could see a Chevy Impala

parked in front of the library. So either Brittany was alive or her husband had driven six hundred miles an hour to get there first.

Cora went into the bakeshop to find Brittany very much alive and pissed as hell.

"You weren't here," Brittany said. "You were supposed to be here."

"Here I am," Cora said.

"You know how long I've been waiting?"

"Am I supposed to guess?"

"It's not funny. How are you going to protect me if you're not here?"

"But so many people are," Cora said. "And you're kind of making a scene in front of them. Did you get a scone? Yes, I can see you did. I'm going to get one, too, and we can take them outside."

Cora bought herself a scone and a latte and guided Brittany outside. "Now what do you say we take your car out to your house?"

"What about your car?"

"If I'm parked in front of the house, your husband will know I'm there. If I'm not, he won't."

"That's your brilliant plan?" Brittany said.

"Well, it beats doing nothing. The guy tries to kill you, I pop out, blow his head off."

"How will you know if he's trying to kill me?"

"Well, I'm not going to ask him. Guys in that position usually lie. 'Kill her? Naw, I just popped in a for a quickie.' What do I do then? Apologize and say 'go for it'?"

"And what am I going to be doing during all this?" Brittany said.

"Actually, you don't need to be there at all. Why don't I drop you at the mall. You can go shopping, and I'll do my best Big-Bad-Wolf-who-just-ate-Grandma impression."

"You're going to leave me alone in the mall?"

"Why not? He won't know you're there."

"Unless he's watching when you let me out."

"You think I couldn't spot him?"

"I don't want to bet my life on it. Look, this is getting out of hand. I don't want you to kill my husband. I just want you to keep him from killing me."

"And the surest way to do that is to catch him in the act."

"That doesn't sound good to me. That sounds bad to me. That's like using me for bait. I don't wanna be bait. I wanna be protected, not put at risk. But I like your other idea."

"What other idea?"

"The mall."

"You'll hang out at the mall and let me handle your husband?"

"What, leave me alone? No, that's an awful idea. You gotta stick with me."

Cora frowned. "So?"

"So. Whaddya say?" Brittany smiled. "Let's go to the mall."

Becky was amused. "You spent the morning at the mall?"

"Yes, we did," Brittany said brightly.

Cora said nothing, but from the look on her face, Becky figured she'd better change the subject. "Well, I hope you girls had fun. Let's get down to business. The deadline for the blackmail is up this afternoon. Now where do we stand on that?"

"The blackmail's off. I called Melvin last night," Cora said.

That was the short version of the story. The long version was Melvin saw no reason not to collect the ten thousand dollars just because Cora had arbitrarily decided not to go through with the bluff. It had not been easy to dissuade him, and Cora wasn't sure he wouldn't go through with it. He'd given his word, but she knew what that was worth.

"How are you handling that?" Brittany said. "Blackmailer changed his mind? You don't think that will make him suspicious?"

"Oh, pooh," Cora said. "According to you, *everything* makes this guy suspicious. So what do you want now, you want me to black-mail him so he won't be suspicious?"

"Of course not."

"So that's the situation. The deadline's gonna pass; absolutely nothing's gonna happen. Your husband will be nervous and irri-table, particularly if he spent the day raising ten thousand dollars. However, given that situation and the state of uncertainty, you think he's gonna try to kill you?"

"I don't know what to think."

"Well, I do. You can't have me living at your house without—are you ready for it—making your husband suspicious. So, you're at a crossroads. Your lawyer can explain your options. If I were you, I'd listen."

Becky smiled. "No, you're on a roll. You tell her, Cora."

"Okay," Cora said. "You can pretend nothing happened, and hope Hubby doesn't kill you. Or you can confront the situation head-on. In any of a number of ways. Would you like to hear what they are? If the answer is no, I don't see any reason for my further employment."

"What ways?" Brittany said through clenched teeth.

Cora ticked them off on her fingers. "One, you ask to see the in-surance policy. We can make up a plausible excuse why you need to if you decide to do it. Two, you confront your husband about his girlfriend. Again, we can come up with a reason why you suspect. Lipstick on a collar, the smell of perfume, just the fact he stays out late. But trust me, if you wanna go that way, I can get more specific. I'm an expert at this. Three, you're concerned for your safety; you think someone means to harm you. You would think that would be harder to sell, but actually, it has the advantage of being true. As-suming it is. Which in itself will lend an air of authenticity. The man immediately feels guilty. Good God, how was he found out? Where did he slip up? What does she know? The fact you're making it up will get lost in the shuffle."

"Are those the only alternatives?"

"There's another. You move out of the house and file suit for divorce."

Brittany's mouth fell open. "Are you serious? If I do that, he's going to really want to kill me."

"If you don't like that, there's only one more option."

"I thought that was the last option."

"Naw. I saved the best for last."

"What's that?"

"Go to the police."

Chief Harper regarded the three women suspiciously. It was not often townspeople requested to see him in his office. When they did, bringing a lawyer was a red flag. Bringing Cora Felton was a flashing neon sign.

"You want to see me?" Harper said. He addressed the remark to Brittany, though realizing the chance she would be the one answering would be next to nil.

"That's right," Becky said. "This woman has something to tell you. It's rather delicate. It requires complete discretion."

Harper rubbed his forehead, wondered why he'd gotten out of bed. Nothing ever happened in Bakerhaven, except when it did, in which case all hell usually broke loose. And Cora Felton was usually at the bottom of it. This, he realized, wasn't quite fair. Cora wasn't the catalyst for such incidents, though she seemed to always be involved. In fact, she was often at the heart of the matter, the central player. The problem to be overcome. With Cora in the mix, it was best to tread lightly.

"Yes?" he said, hoping the question mark would render the statement noncommittal.

"So we may count on your cooperation?" Becky persisted.

"I can't promise you anything. I don't know what you're talking about. If you don't have something to say, please remember I gave you this opportunity. I would not like to see a TV interview where you claim you went to the police and they wouldn't listen."

"My God," Brittany said. "Is everyone in town crazy, or paranoid, or what? I'd like to talk to you about my husband without worrying you're going to turn around and tell him. Is that simple enough?"

Harper hesitated. In the back of his mind was the nagging doubt there could be a dozen ways that wouldn't be simple enough and Cora and Becky would be sure to come up with every one of them.

On the other hand, he wasn't under oath. "I wasn't planning on running to your husband. What's the problem?"

"Let me serve up a hypothetical," Becky said. Harper groaned. Becky ignored it, went on as if there'd been no interruption. "If her husband were thinking of committing a crime and she informed you of that fact, would you feel obliged to act on it?"

"If you tell me he's going to rob the bank I'm not going to sit back and watch him do it."

"Of course not. But you don't have to tell him his wife ratted him out."

Chief Harper sighed. "What's this all about?"

"She thinks her husband's trying to kill her," Cora said.

Becky and Brittany glared at her.

"Come on," Cora said. "We're never going to get anywhere this way. Here's the thing. Her husband bought a double-indemnity life insurance policy. He's got a young floozy in the City. Two million bucks would furnish a pretty nice love nest."

Harper scowled. "That's the situation?"

"That's it in a nutshell."

"What do you expect me to do about it?"

"Don't let it happen."

"And how do you expect me to do that? You don't want me to confront the husband. I assume you're not asking for police protection."

"No, but police *presence* would be nice."

"What do you mean?"

"Well," Cora said. "The guy moved in here less than a year ago. There must be some town ordinance he's violating. Or at least something you need to check into. So when he gets home from work his wife can say, 'The police were looking for you.' Not the type of thing a killer wants to hear."

"This is absurd," Harper said. "Do you have anything more to go on than what you've given me?"

"No," Cora said. The fact that she and Melvin had tried to blackmail the husband seemed rather irrelevant.

Harper sighed. It had been such a calm day. Officer Finley had caught a speeder out by the bypass, but that had been it. He rubbed his forehead, cleared his throat.

"Okay."

An explosion blew out the windows of the police station.

Outside was a scene of chaos. People were piling from the buildings to see what was going on. In front of the library, a car was on fire. Flames were shooting up to the sky. The whole car appeared to be consumed. The fire roared and crackled; the heat could be felt all the way across the street.

With the fire raging out of control it was impossible to identify the vehicle, but Cora had a good idea whose car it was. She and Brittany had left it parked there and gone to the mall in her own, so if by the slimmest of chances Brittany's husband had driven by the mall he wouldn't have seen her car and known she was there. On the other hand, the thought of his searching the library all morning had been rather pleasant.

That was then and this was now. Brittany's car was a raging inferno. If there was a person in all those flames, it was an entirely different ball game indeed.

Cora squeezed Becky's arm. "Get her upstairs."

"Huh?"

"That's her car, and she's about to have a meltdown. Get her out of here before she does."

Becky nodded, grabbed the distraught woman, and skillfully guided her away.

Cora turned back to the scene. Crept as close as she could to the car without being burned. She was still quite a distance away but a lot nearer than the rest of the mob in the street.

"Stay back!" Dan Finley warned.

Dan had managed to grab a yellow crime scene ribbon and was cordoning off the area. It wasn't easy. There was nothing to anchor the ribbon to without running it across the street. Dan had improvised by backing his cruiser out from the police station and parking it closer to the fire than was probably prudent. He'd rolled down the windows and managed to run the ribbon in the front and out the back. It made for a pretty effective hitching post, but the cruiser was going to fill up with soot.

Cora ducked back behind the ribbon, continued to creep around the car.

"There's someone in it."

Cora looked.

A teenage boy had ducked under the ribbon and was pointing at the front seat. Dan Finley immediately chased him away, but the damage had been done. There did indeed appear to be a body in the front seat, and everyone was pointing at it.

Cora wasn't surprised, but she wasn't pleased, either. Cora had expected to find a body in the car but wanted to keep it quiet as long as possible. Now people would be calling the TV stations. Though Dan Finley had probably tipped off Rick Reed at Channel Eight already.

Aaron Grant pushed his way through the crowd. Sherry Carter's young husband had run from his office at the *Bakerhaven Gazette* without stopping to grab his coat. "You see it happen?"

Cora shook her head. "I came up after. I was in the police station, heard it, and ran out."

"Did anyone?"

"I don't know."

"Whose car?"

"I'm not sure."

Aaron scowled. "Damn it, TV will be here any minute. What can you give me?"

"You getting out an extra?"

"Not my call." Aaron lowered his voice. "You got anything you're not giving them?"

"That I'd want to see in the press?"

"Yeah, I know. Just give me whatever you can."

"Will do."

Cora disappeared in the crowd. She felt bad about holding out on Aaron, but at this point there was nothing she could say. If the car was Brittany's, the ensuing questions would get ugly. Becky would step in, and all hell would break loose. It would be a toss-up whether Brittany was cast as a victim or a perpetrator.

Cora started around the car in the other direction, where Sam Brogan was being harangued by Fred Burns from the hardware store and Judy Douglas Knauer, the real estate agent, who apparently owned the cars parked next to the flaming wreck. Parking in front of the library was head-in, so not only were the cars next to it at risk, but it was way too hot to move either of them. Cora wasn't sure just what Sam Brogan was supposed to do about it, but she knew the cranky officer would have a lot to say on the subject later.

Cora spotted Barney Nathan in the crowd. Dapper as ever in his red bow tie, the doctor had run from his office in mid-examination. His patient wasn't complaining; she'd run out to see what was happening, too.

Cora weaved her way over to Barney. He looked guilty to see her, as he always did since they'd broken off their brief affair. At least brief by her standards. It being Barney's first affair, he found the whole thing momentous.

"Hey, Barney. Got a minute?"

Barney looked like he'd been propositioned in the street. "What do you want?"

"The body's toast. You're not getting near it anytime soon. Whaddya say you make yourself useful?"

Barney just gawked. Cora put her arm around his shoulders, which undoubtedly added to his discomfit. "The woman whose car blew up is hysterical. The charcoal briquette in the front seat is probably her husband. You think you could check her out, see if she needs a sedative? She's in pretty bad shape."

"Where is she?"

"Up in Becky Baldwin's office."

Barney gave her a look.

"She had nothing to do with it, Barney. She was actually in the police station when it happened."

"The police station?"

"Of her own accord," Cora said impatiently. "She was talking to Harper; there was an explosion outside. You can ask the chief."

"All right. As soon as EMS gets here I'll check her out."

"They're not going to be able to get near the body, either."

"Maybe not. I still have to tell them what I want done. Don't worry, I'll be up."

Relieved she wasn't hitting on him, Barney escaped into the crowd.

Cora continued her inspection of the crime scene. There were still several cars parked in front of the library. None were close enough to the fire to be in danger, and no one had wanted to drive off. Cora checked them out and stopped dead.

Brittany's car was parked there. At least it looked like Brittany's car. Was that where she parked, or was it two spaces over? When Cora'd come back from chasing Brittany's husband she'd noted the car was there, figured Brittany was already in the bakeshop. But as to exactly where it was parked, Cora couldn't have sworn to it.

The license plate was JRV 715. Was that Brittany's or Hank's? She had no idea. Some detective.

Chief Harper came walking up. "There's a body in the car."

"So I understand."

"Who is it?"

"I was hoping you could tell me. Burned beyond recognition?"

"Looks like it."

"Can't help you, Chief."

"Funny thing it happens while you're in my office asking for help."

"You find that funny?"

"I find it suspicious."

"Suspicious of what? I assure you I had nothing to do with that fire."

"Maybe not directly."

"Directly, indirectly, I—"

An explosion rocked the street. People dived for cover. Even Cora and the chief were on the ground. An unpleasant experience. The fire had melted the snow and ice, creating a holy mess. Cora clambered to her feet, wiped the slush off her face. Chief Harper had a streak of mud across his.

"Damn," Harper said.

Cora cocked her head. "I don't suppose that's going to help the identification any."

Cora burst into Becky's office. "What's the plate number on your car?"

Brittany looked annoyed. "Huh?"

"Your license plate. What's the number?"

"Why?"

"There's two Chevy Impalas in front of the library, and I want to know if the one burning is yours."

Brittany gasped. "You mean . . . ?"

"Yes, I mean," Cora said. "If it's your car, there's some question as to whether that body in the front seat is Hank. If it's his car . . ."

Brittany's eyes were wide. She looked on the verge of hysterics. "I don't understand."

"You and me both, sister. One way or another Chief Harper's going to be up here asking questions." Cora turned to Becky. "You gonna want your client to answer?"

Becky looked at Brittany. "What's your license number?"

"I-I-"

"Snap out of it," Cora said. "You think these questions are tough?

Wait'll Chief Harper starts asking. I'll make it easy for you. Is your number JRV seven-one-five?"

"No. That's Hank's car."

"Good. Your car blew up. Your husband's car's parked nearby. It looks like he tried to put a car bomb in your glove compartment and it blew up on him. Which will let you off the hook."

"Maybe so," Becky said, "but you're not telling your story yet."

"Why not?"

"There's too many things we don't know."

"Don't sugarcoat it, Becky," Cora said. "Your husband's dead. If it wasn't an accident, you're the chief suspect. The wife always is. Keep quiet till you know the score."

"Won't that make me look guilty?"

"Don't worry," Becky said. "You're not refusing to answer questions; you're just too upset. It's been a huge shock."

There was a knock on the door.

"Remember," Becky said, "if that's the police, I'm making all the statements."

It was Dr. Nathan with his medical bag.

"Oh, hi, Barney," Cora said. "Brittany, do you know Dr. Nathan? I asked him to stop in and see if you needed help. Barney, she's very upset. The dead man is probably her husband."

Barney took a stethoscope out of his bag, smiled at Brittany. "Okay, Brittany. Take a breath. Relax as much as you can. Put yourself in my hands."

"Sure thing, Doc," Cora said. "We'll leave you to it."

Cora herded Becky out the door.

"What the hell?" Becky said. "Who put you in charge?"

"Sorry, but we need to talk. You can soft-pedal this all you want, but Chief Harper is not happy about the fact it happened while we were in his office making a claim against the selfsame husband who was just blown to kingdom come."

"She claimed he was trying to kill her."

"Yes, and isn't that just too pat. She cast her husband in the role of the killer, then kills him so it looks like he accidently killed himself."

"And just how does she do that?"

"Damned if I know. But you think the police aren't going to think so?"

"It may cross Harper's mind. But he'd have a tough time proving it."

"Maybe. But wouldn't it be better if he never makes the accusation? It would certainly be better for me. I would hate to find myself on the witness stand testifying to what I did in the wife's defense. 'Miss Felton, did you have any personal involvement with the decedent?' 'You mean besides blackmailing him for ten thousand dollars?'"

"I see your point."

"You better go check on Barney, see that he gives her some whacking big dose of powerful sedative."

"What are you going to do?"

Cora's eyes were hard. "Look for a scapegoat."

Mrs. Cushman had dragged a folding table out of the bakeshop and put out a coffee urn for the firemen. Hot coffee to a fire might have seemed redundant, but it was cold outside. Bakerhaven had only one fire truck. There were six volunteers but usually only two or three at a time, depending on the severity of the fire. Considering the spectacular nature of the blaze, today they were all there, taking turns on the hoses and the coffee table.

Cora found Kevin Graves dumping cream in a Styrofoam cup. Kevin was a barber who worked during the day and generally answered calls at night. Today, he'd run from his shop in mid-haircut. Somewhere in the crowd was a spectator with half-trimmed hair.

Cora sidled up to the table. "Hey, Kevin, what's the scoop?"

Kevin himself was remarkably unkempt for a barber. He favored her with a lopsided smile. "What do you mean?"

"Any ideas about the fire?"

"Why do you ask?"

"My niece married a reporter. I like to help the kids out."

"I don't want to be quoted."

Cora realized she'd taken the wrong tack, immediately tried to backtrack. "I'm not going to quote you. Promise. I won't even say where this came from. Any ideas?"

"Word is it's a car bomb. Guy started the car, blew himself up."

"In Bakerhaven?"

Kevin grinned. "Yeah, I know. Seems out of place, but that's what it looks like."

"What if it wasn't? What would you think then?"

He frowned. "What do you mean?"

"The car caught fire. If it wasn't a bomb, what could it have been?"

"I don't know. Who burns a car?"

"Who burns anything?" Cora said. "Say it wasn't a car, say it was just a fire, what would you think then?"

"Oh, that's easy," Kevin said. He stopped himself. "You're *not* quoting me on this."

"I told you I wasn't."

"Well, you didn't hear it from me. But everybody knows."

"Knows what?"

"Billy Wilson."

"Who?"

"You don't know Billy Wilson? Of course, you're not a volunteer." Kevin raised his head, looked around. "Ah. See the man over there, far side of the street? The guy watching the fire, seems to be enjoying it a little too much? Billy the Bug."

At Cora's puzzled look Kevin said, "Firebug. Busted three or four times. He's had jail, parole, community service, psychiatric counseling. Finally took. Hasn't torched a place in ten years. But if you asked me who'd have done it, that's what I'd have said."

"Ten years?"

"Give or take. Not that we haven't had fires since then. They just weren't arson."

"Interesting," Cora said.

Kevin threw his coffee cup in the garbage, went back to work another shift.

Cora worked her way through the crowd to a position from which she could better assess Billy Wilson. She studied him through the smoke and the flickering flames. He'd certainly gotten as close as he could go, was actually pushing against the crime scene ribbon. Billy was a chubby little man with a round face but tiny nose. He wore a red parka, open at the front with the hood down, probably because he was so close to the fire. The coat had lots of deep pockets, useful in concealing lighters and accelerants.

What Kevin had said opened up interesting possibilities. There'd been no cases of arson in the last ten years. From that Kevin concluded that Billy'd reformed.

It occurred to Cora there was another possibility.

Maybe he'd just gotten better at it.

Chief Harper found Cora in the crowd, fixed her with an evil eye. "I suppose this is your doing."

"Oh, hi, Chief. What's my doing?"

"I just tried to interview Brittany Wells. But I couldn't do it, because Barney Nathan gave her some sort of horse tranquilizer. I'd be surprised if she wakes up by Wednesday."

"Good idea. She seemed upset."

"As if I didn't know *whose* idea."

"Wednesday was *your* idea, Chief." Cora raised her eyebrows. "So. You question him yet?"

"Who?"

"Billy the Bug. I hear you busted him quite a few times in the past."

Harper waved it away. "This wasn't Billy Wilson."

"Are you sure?"

"Don't be silly."

"Why is that silly? If it were a rape, would you be looking at sex offenders?"

"That's different."

"In what way?"

Chief Harper flushed. "He burned houses, not cars."

"He couldn't have diversified?"

"You shouldn't be doing this, Cora."

"Doing what?"

"It's a red flag. You're afraid I'll pick on the wife, so you're throwing me a red herring."

"Not at all. One of the firemen told me you had a local firebug, so I thought I'd pass it on. But if you're telling me it means nothing . . ."

"Absolutely nothing. Zero. Zilch. You're on the wrong track."

"Good to know." Cora pointed. "Oh, look. Rick Reed's here."

Harper muttered something under his breath.

"Nice quote, Chief. I'm sure Rick will love it."

Rick Reed of Channel Eight News was holding forth in front of the blazing wreck. Even with the crime scene cordoned off, the news team had managed to find an angle in the street that put the flames in the background.

"Car bomb in Bakerhaven!" Rick boldly proclaimed, though no one had determined that was what it was. "The quiet streets of Bakerhaven were rocked just an hour ago when a car parked outside the library suddenly exploded and burst into flames, killing the driver, who had just started the car," he continued, possibly establishing a record for the number of assumptions stated as fact in a single sentence. Whether or not the explosion was the result of a car bomb, there was no evidence as to whether the car was running, whether the driver had started the car, whether the ignition had triggered the bomb, or whether the ensuing blast had killed the man or woman in the front seat, if there indeed was a person in the inferno. The charred corpse, if that's what it was, had not been moved, let along examined. The EMS unit stood by the ambulance, waiting for the Bakerhaven volunteer fire department to put out the fire. Till then, no one was eager to go close to the vehicle.

Cora moved through the crowd and wandered injudiciously close to Rick Reed, who had paused for a commercial. He spotted her and pounced.

"Cora! Glad I caught you. Can I get you on camera?"

"Sorry, Rick. Don't have time. But I don't know anything yet, anyway."

"Nothing at all?"

"No. Oh, well, I understand Chief Harper ruled out the local firebug."

"The local firebug?"

"So I hear."

"Who's the local firebug?"

"Oh, was that before your time? I hear it's a while ago. I think it's before mine. At least I never knew. And it's the sort of thing you'd think you'd hear."

"Who are we talking about?"

"Oh, I don't know. Doesn't mean anything, anyway. The chief says there's nothing to it."

Cora moved off before Rick could ask a follow-up. Out of the corner of her eye she could see him scanning the crowd for Chief Harper.

Cora went back to Becky's office, where the young attorney was riding herd over her client. Brittany was sitting in a chair. She wasn't sleeping, but she wasn't responsive, either. Her eyes were glazed.

"I understand Chief Harper was up here."

"Yeah. He wasn't happy."

"I'm not surprised. Looks like Barney did a nice job."

"I suppose I have you to thank for that."

"It seemed like a good idea at the time."

"Absolutely. She's a lot more fun to be with. Except she might fall over. Listen, you want to babysit for a while? It's my first car bomb."

"Actually, no one's calling it that yet. Except Rick Reed."

"He's here?"

"Yeah. You feel like being interviewed?"

"Why not? I look good on TV."

"What you gonna say?"

"'No comment.'"

"Not exactly enlightening."

"No, but I look good saying it."

"Yes, you do."

"So will you babysit?"

Cora sized Brittany up. "I should probably drive her home."

"She's certainly in no shape to do it."

"Yeah, but that's not why."

"Oh? Why?"

"She hasn't got a car."

Cora took Brittany home, put her to sleep in the upstairs bedroom. Brittany offered little resistance. Dr. Nathan had done a good job. Cora tucked her in, turned out the light, and closed the door.

Then she went downstairs and ransacked the study.

There was an old oak desk with many drawers. Some had keyholes, but none were locked, which was disappointing. A locked drawer would be much more promising.

Cora went through all the papers as if she had every right to do so. She figured in a way, she did. Cora was Becky's representative. Becky was Brittany's attorney. Brittany's husband was dead, and Brittany was his beneficiary. It was therefore necessary to inventory his property in order to conserve the estate.

And if Chief Harper bought that one she should probably try her luck at the state lottery.

Cora finished up her search of the desk having found nothing even remotely interesting except some magazines of a rather suggestive nature. The suggestion was not subtle. It was, however, the type of thing that would have appealed to Melvin. It occurred to

Cora she needed to apprise Melvin of the latest development before he did anything foolish. It also occurred to her it would be prudent not to call from Brittany's phone.

The file cabinet next to the desk looked promising and did indeed hold several family-related documents, such as the rental agreement and the electric, gas, cable, and phone bills.

There were also statements from the local bank. According to the latest, Hank Wells had expired with approximately sixteen thousand dollars in his account. Not princely, but a useful sum for a young widow with mounting attorney's fees.

One drawer was locked. Cora wondered if she should wake Brittany up and get the keys. Assuming Brittany *had* the keys. Which seemed a long shot, all things considered. Most likely, the only one with keys to the file cabinet was Hank.

In which case, they probably just blew up.

Sherry met Cora at the door with Jennifer on her hip. "A car blew up and you're involved."

"Not exactly how I'd have phrased it." Cora pushed by Sherry and went in. "You ever use your end of the house?'

"This is more homey."

"You noticed." Cora went into the kitchen.

"Where you going?"

"I need some coffee."

"Want me to make it?"

"Thought you'd never ask. Here, give me the troublemaker."

"She's not a troublemaker," Sherry said.

Jennifer squealed. "Troublemaker!" It sounded more like "bubblebaker."

"Now see what you've done," Sherry said. "Jennifer, you're not a troublemaker; you're a good girl."

"A good girl who makes trouble," Cora said. "Come on, Jennifer. Auntie Cora's going to spoil you while Mommy makes coffee."

Cora scooped Jennifer up, whisked her into the living room, and dropped her on the couch. Jennifer squealed in delight.

"Heard that!" Sherry yelled from the kitchen. "If I come in there and find out you're having fun . . ."

"Oh, tough mommy," Cora said. "I'm s-o-o-o scared."

Jennifer giggled.

"Why don't you stop mommy bashing and do something useful."

"Sure. Jennifer, we're going to learn something useful. What do I know that's useful? Ah! Marrying a loser. Jennifer, want to learn how to marry a loser?"

"Wooser!" Jennifer cried.

"I stand corrected," Sherry said, bringing in a steaming cup of coffee. "Don't try to teach her anything useful. Just try not to break her before Aaron gets home."

The poodle came yipping in from Cora's bedroom.

"Hi, Buddy," Cora said. "You didn't come greet me. You're not feeling well?"

"He's fine," Sherry said. "I think Jennifer wore him out."

"I know how he feels." Cora took the cup of coffee, flopped down on the couch. "I'm glad my shift is over."

"It was five minutes," Sherry said.

"Maybe for you. It seemed like an eternity. I'm cranky; I'm irritable."

"You're doing great."

"Yeah, well, I'm done doing it. Now Buddy can do great."

On cue, Jennifer took off after the dog.

Sherry sat down on the couch. "Okay, tell me about the car bomb."

"A car blew up and no one's happy about it."

"I was hoping for a little more than that."

Cora filled her niece in on the situation.

Sherry wasn't impressed. "You don't know any more than Aaron did."

"There's a ringing endorsement. I'll tell him you said so. He may want to blurb it in his bio."

"You *are* cranky, aren't you?"

"Well, I'm less than pleased. Things could hardly be worse."

"At least there's no crossword puzzle."

Cora stood up so fast she spilled her coffee. "Bite your tongue! You don't jinx it when a pitcher's throwing a perfect game. You know when you comment on it? When the last man is out. I got a dead guy in a car and a suspect in a drugged stupor, who better not be guilty, because I'm on her side. That I can handle. I'm climbing the walls, but I can handle it. Throw a crossword puzzle at me and I'm going to freak out."

"Sorry. On a cheerier note, how's the corpse? Was he alive when he burned?"

Cora smiled. "That's my girl. A good question, and one I'm sure Barney Nathan will be answering as soon as he can get close enough to tell. I've never seen a flaming one before. Unless you count my ex-husband Henry."

"Henry's dead?"

"No." Cora sat back down and sipped her coffee. "Anyway, the whole investigation's pretty much on hold because the corpse is inaccessible and the suspect's doped up."

"Where is she?"

"I took her home, put her to sleep."

"Think she'll stay put?"

"She has to. She has no car."

Cora went into her office, logged on to the Internet, began playing Spider Solitaire. She dialed the phone with the other hand.

A gruff voice growled, "Crowley."

Cora growled, "Cora."

"Hey, kid. Whaddya up to?"

"You getting updates from Bakerhaven?"

"No. Should I?"

"Well, probably not, because nobody knows your connection to the case."

A pause. "What case?"

"The car bombing."

"What?"

Cora went through the whole thing again for Crowley. She was getting quite good at it.

"And just how am I involved in all this?" Crowley said.

"Clearly, you aren't," Cora said, "and that's how I'll describe it in my official report."

"Leave me *out* of your official report."

"That will leave some holes in the story."

"What holes? What story?"

"Exactly," Cora said. "Without Hubby's lover, whose identity you so neatly traced for me, I'd have nothing to go on. Though, actually it was Perkins who traced it for me. That's good. Two witnesses are always better than one."

There was another pause. "Are you kidding, or what?"

"Well, if this guy turns out to be a straying husband who accidently did himself in while attempting to bump off his heavily insured wife, then the mistress will go a long way toward establishing that fact. Anyway, the odds are Becky will be sending me to Manhattan to check things out, so I'll give you a call."

"I may be busy."

"You're not very welcoming," Cora said.

"Well, you're threatening to involve me in a murder. I should be jumping up and down?"

"Murder is your business."

"*Solving* them is my business. Taking part in them is not in the job description. The powers that be get very cranky when policemen participate in them."

"The powers that be? That's not just some boogeyman they scare young policemen with?"

"It's exhausting talking to you. I gotta get back to the real world. If you crack the case, let me know."

Crowley hung up the phone.

Cora sat and seethed. Not only had the conversation been unsatisfactory, but she was losing at Spider Solitaire.

Cora was angry with herself. Snap out of it, she thought. Pull yourself together. You're not thinking straight. If you were thinking straight, what would you do?

Well, she wouldn't sit around home playing solitaire while someone else solved the case. She'd go out and beat them to it. And how would she do that? Well, it would help to know what they were doing. Though what Chief Harper was doing in this instance was hard to imagine.

Cora got up to go. Assessed the situation. Okay, before she left the house, was there anything she forgot? Oh, yes.

She dug in her drawstring purse, pulled out an address book, flipped it open, and dialed the number.

He answered on the fourth ring. "Yeah?"

"Melvin? It's Cora."

"Oh? Hi, Cora."

"Listen. About the blackmail."

"Yeah?"

"I'm afraid I have bad news."

The street in front of the library was still smoldering, but the fire had been put out and the car towed away. Dan Finley's cruiser was also gone. The crime scene ribbon was now supported by four small stanchions, though what it was meant to protect Cora had no idea. There was nothing left but ash.

Cora pushed up the steps into the police station.

Dan Finley was at his desk. His eyes widened, and he shook his head and waved his hands in a warning gesture.

"I take it the chief's in his office."

"Good guess. You might wanna come back later."

Cora smiled, went on in.

Chief Harper was on the phone. He said, "Call you back," slammed it down, and lunged to his feet. He seemed to be fighting to control his temper.

"What's up, Chief? You don't look happy."

"I was just interviewed by Rick Reed," he said through clenched teeth.

"Oh," Cora said. "And you had nothing to tell him because you couldn't question the widow."

"That's not it and you know it."

"Oh?"

"Don't 'oh' me. I already bawled you out for getting Barney to drug your client."

"Actually, she's Becky's client."

"Don't do that. I'm not in the mood."

"What's the matter, Chief?"

"You know damn well what's the matter. Rick Reed just shoved a microphone in my face. And you know what he wants to talk about?"

"Knowing Rick, it could be anything."

"Billy Wilson, that's what. He wants to know how I'm so sure this isn't the work of Billy the Bug."

"And is it?"

Harper's eyes blazed. "*You* know it isn't; *I* know it isn't; *the whole world* knows it isn't. But somehow Rick Reed got the idea I'd been looking into it. You wouldn't know how that happened?"

"Like you say, Chief, who knows why Rick Reed does anything?"

"I do," Harper said. "In this case I do. I know why he does it. I know exactly why he does it. Seeing as how you asked me the identical question just this afternoon."

"Gee, Chief, if everyone's talking about it, maybe there's something to it."

Harper's face was red. A vein in his forehead was beginning to resemble a baseball bat. "Not when all of that talk can be traced back to you. Look, I don't have time for this. Change the subject or get out of my office."

"Well, since you asked me so nicely. What are you working on, Chief, that leaves you no time for my theories?"

"I have time for your theories. Just not that one."

"Only one I got, Chief. And it's not my theory. Some fireman mentioned it."

Harper waved it away. "Yeah, yeah. Moving on. Anyway, the widow's drugged and Becky's not talking. Hell of a situation. On the one hand, a prime suspect isn't talking. On the other, she isn't *refusing* to talk."

"Which I'm sure you pointed out to Becky."

"Yes, I did. She'd love to help me, but she can't violate a client's confidence."

"Of course not."

"But you can. You have to. You have no legal right to hold out. In fact, if you do you're guilty of obstructing justice."

"Come on, Chief. Couldn't you just ask nicely?"

"Not when you're waving firebugs in my face. All right, look. We checked out Hubby's office in the city. He's not there."

"That's a bad sign."

"No kidding. His coworkers don't seem to have known him well. He's been at the firm less than a year. His work was steady, but not inspired."

"An insurance salesman not inspiring. I'm shocked."

"As for taking out insurance on his wife, if he did, it wasn't with them. There's no record of any such policy."

"No insurance policy. Gee, I guess the wife didn't have such a good motive for killing him. Oh, wait a minute. The policy's on her. So it wasn't a good motive anyway. Gee, Chief, I don't see why you can't wash the wife out entirely."

"I probably would if people weren't so eager to pump her full of drugs. It seems like a guilty reaction to me."

"Or a normal reaction when dealing with a spouse who's had a traumatic shock."

"Anyway, if there's a policy we can't find it. As for the other woman, we can't find her, either. No one at the firm suspected he had a girlfriend. Or if they did, they're not letting on. At any rate, we can't find her. Which brings me to you."

"Ah," Cora said. "This is where you want me to betray confidential information you can't get from Becky Baldwin."

"There is where I want you to divulge relevant information you have no legal right to withhold."

"Mind if I consult Becky about that?"

"Why in the world would you have to?"

"You said something about obstruction of justice. Last I checked, that's a crime. If you suspect me of a crime, I'm consulting an attorney."

"Fine. I just spoke to Becky. She's in her office. Call her and ask her."

"Not with you listening, and not on your phone. I'll run up and be right back."

Becky's office was down the side street over a pizza parlor. It occurred to Cora the pepperoni smelled awfully good.

Becky was at her desk. "Hi, Cora. What's up?"

"Harper wants me to rat out the mistress."

"What's the problem?"

"I didn't think you'd want me to."

Becky shrugged. "I can't stop you. If he wants the information, he's entitled to it."

"That's not good. She might mention Hubby was being blackmailed."

"That's entirely likely. You think it might have been wiser *not* to blackmail him?"

"In hindsight, it probably would."

"In any circumstances I can think of, it probably would. If he wants to know, you have to tell him. I don't suppose you could head off Melvin so he doesn't walk in while the cops are there."

"Already did."

"How'd he take it?"

"Remember when you found out there was no Santa Claus?"

"Sure. It was just last week. Listen, I'd be a lot more worried if there were any chance my client had anything to do with this. Aside from no motive, we were talking to the chief when it happened. The only downside here is anything illegal you might have done.

Until Chief Harper gets wind of it, let's not point him in the right direction by claiming you're my client and refusing to answer questions."

"Right," Cora said.

Becky looked at her. "Cora, you know all this. You don't need my advice. You could have handled Chief Harper on your own."

"I don't want to compromise your position."

"Never stopped you before. What's the matter? Melvin make you nervous?"

"Not at all," Cora said irritably. She got up, went out the door.

Cora reported back to Chief Harper. "Okay, I got clearance. On two occasions I followed the gentleman in question from his place of business to a young lady's apartment. I never saw the woman, but I know she was there on at least one occasion, because I saw her arm close the living room blind. And on both occasions someone buzzed him in."

"You never saw the woman?"

"That's right."

"I find that hard to believe. I'm surprised you didn't bang on her door."

"I was told not to."

"And you always do what you're told."

"I did this time. You wanna fault me on it."

"Got a name and address?"

Cora gave it to him.

"Okay, I'll run it by the NYPD. Who's that cop you're palsy with?"

"I beg your pardon?'

"Well, it's not my jurisdiction, and I don't have time to do it myself." Harper snatched up the phone. "Hey, Dan. You know that New York cop friend of Cora's. Get him on the phone, see if he can go see a woman for us." He gave Dan the name and address. "It's got to be in person. It's the girlfriend. She won't know he's dead."

"You don't know he's dead," Cora said. "All you've got is a charred corpse."

"Yeah, but we're all friends here. We don't have to say 'alleged' every time we refer to the victim."

Cora left the police station in a foul mood. She should have seen that coming. Of course Harper wouldn't check out the girl himself. And who better than Crowley? She should have warned him. Not that he couldn't handle it himself. But he'd be pissed. Cora didn't need anyone pissed at her. Particularly not Crowley.

Damn.

Chapter

3 4

The phone rang while Cora was in the bath. Cora hated that. For obvious reasons. And for some less than obvious ones. For one thing, it pointed up the fact that the nationally famous Puzzle Lady didn't have a phone in her bathroom. A lot of celebrities did. Cora thought it was pretty stupid. She could think of a lot of places she'd rather make a call. On the other hand, not having to spring out of the bathtub and run dripping into the other room to answer the phone would be a hell of a plus.

Cora wondered if there was anyone she wanted to talk to badly enough to do that. Unfortunately, there were a couple of pending phone calls she needed to take. If it was Crowley in a snit, she didn't dare miss it.

Cora lunged to her feet, cascades of water shedding from her body as if she were a dolphin at SeaWorld. It occurred to her she had consciously used the image of a dolphin so as not to use the image of Shamu. Cora had put on a couple of pounds lately, making her more than usually self-conscious. She grabbed a towel, wrapped it around her, plunged down the hall.

It wasn't the phone in the office; it was the phone in her bedroom. Was that good or bad? She had no idea. It occurred to her for the zillionth time she ought to get caller ID. She plunked down on the bed, picked up the phone. "Hello?"

"Cora, it's Chief Harper. I need your help."

"You're a big man to admit it, Chief."

"I can't get Crowley. He's gone for the day and can't be reached. I left a message. He hasn't called back."

"Can't someone else check it out for you?'

"Thought you'd never ask."

"Whoa! I didn't mean me."

"Why not? You know where she lives."

"Not the sort of thing I want to let her know."

"I'm sure you'll have no problem prevaricating."

"Prevaricating? Did you really say 'prevaricating'?"

"I try to load up on big words when I'm talking to you."

"Can't someone else do it?"

"Come on, Cora. I'd like to keep it in the family. And if this woman's the mistress, she may not be eager to claim the relationship. In which case you'll do a better job than your average cop."

"Now there's a recommendation: 'better than your average cop.' I'll put it on my résumé. You know who else will love it? Cops. It'll leave 'em with a warm, fuzzy glow."

"I can't believe you don't want to do this. Usually, I can't stop you from butting in."

"You're full of flattery today, aren't you? Relax, Chief; I'll check it out."

Cora hung up on the chief and called Becky Baldwin. "Harper wants me to check out the other woman."

"What's wrong with that?"

"I don't want her to tell me about the blackmail. I wouldn't want to withhold it from the chief, but I'd have a hard time telling him with a straight face."

"See? This is why blackmail is not always a good idea."

"I'll keep that in mind. Anyway, I'm heading for the City."

"Coming back?"

"Not if I can help it."

Cora threw on some clothes and went out. Aaron was home, so she wasn't leaving Sherry stranded. Of course it might have been nice to let her know where she was going, but she didn't want to advertise the fact, what with Aaron being a reporter and all.

Cora drove down the Merritt Parkway and plotted her strategy. Never mind what Chief Harper would make of the answers, what was this woman going to think of the questions? What reason in the world could Cora give her for investigating the crime? "Hi, I'm a crossword constructor and I may or may not have bad news for you. A man you know may have been killed. Just what *is* your relationship with the possible corpse?" That didn't seem too promising. Cora knew she could do it better, but that wasn't going to help. All the tact and diplomacy in the world couldn't alter the fact that she was inquiring into things that were none of her business.

Snap out of it, she told herself. Look on the bright side. You're not a cop, so you don't have to give her a Miranda warning. You can ask any damn thing you want, and she has no legal recourse.

Except to sue her. For exactly what Cora wasn't sure, but a lawyer would be able to find grounds.

Cora beat herself up for most of the drive and came to one conclusion. Actually, she came to several conclusions, but the one she flip-flopped back to by the time she hit Manhattan was that the interview would go much better if someone else conducted it. And while Chief Harper might have wanted her to question the woman, she was actually his second choice. He'd only asked her because Crowley wasn't answering his phone.

From experience, Cora knew Crowley didn't answer his cell phone when he was home.

She also knew where he lived.

Instead of getting off the West Side Highway at 79th Street, Cora took it downtown to the West Village. She got off at 18th Street and began the series of loops and turns she had come to know well. From her few months with Crowley, Cora knew the confusing

Greenwich Village streets like the back of her hand, and could navigate with nary a flick of an eye intersections such as 10th Street crossing 4th Street, doubtless dreamed up by some diabolical demon from hell expressly for the purpose of freaking potheads out.

Cora swooped around the final curve, found a parking spot right on Crowley's block. As she went up the front steps of his brownstone apartment, she wondered should she do this? Was she being presumptuous? Not after the day before. There's welcoming and there's welcoming. With one's clothes scattered in all directions, it was impossible to misconstrue. No, he'd be happy to see her, even if she did need a favor. Not that interviewing the woman was a big deal. He'd have already done it if Harper had been able to reach him.

Cora hesitated a moment, rang the bell.

There was no answer. No buzz unlocking the door. No gruff voice asking to know who it was.

Cora figured she should give him a minute. Maybe he was in the john. She waited a minute, buzzed again.

The door was pushed open by a middle-aged woman. She was tall and thin, with straight straw-colored hair and faded freckles on her cheeks. She smiled. "You're Cora Felton, aren't you? I've seen you on TV. Do come in."

Cora frowned. "I don't understand."

"Oh. Crowley's out. He doesn't like me to buzz people in without seeing who they are. I mean, there's only so much you can tell over an intercom."

"Who are you?" Cora said.

"Oh, I'm sorry. I know you. But we've never met." She smiled. "I'm Stephanie."

Cora sat on the couch sipping tea. It occurred to her the living room was the only place in the apartment she had never spent any time.

"I've known him since college," Stephanie said. "My goodness, seems like yesterday, and now look. He went off and became a policeman, and got married, and it didn't last. I never got out of the sixties, really. Had a tapestry shop on Bleecker. Still do. But the product's changed. Along with the clientele. It's draperies now. Interior designers."

Cora felt like her head was coming off. "Did you ever get married?" she asked.

"Once. To a kindergarten teacher in the public school system. Turned out he didn't like children. Not that he didn't want to have them. He didn't like the ones he taught. Turned into a grouch. I stood it for three years, threw in the towel."

"You're Crowley's girlfriend," Cora said.

Stephanie smiled. "I'm his friend."

"His ex-wife seemed to think you were his girlfriend."

"Yes. She would. But we're really just friends."

"Friends with benefits."

Stephanie grimaced. "I hate that expression. It's after our time, you know what I mean?"

"What expression do you like?"

She shrugged. "We're friends."

There came the sound of the key in the lock. Crowley walked in, saw the women sitting on the couch, and stopped dead. His mouth hung open. He looked like a trout about to be reeled in.

"Hi, Crowley," Cora said. "Sit down; have some tea. Stephanie was just telling me about your sex life."

Stephanie laughed. "You're very wicked. You didn't tell me she was wicked."

"What are you doing here?" Crowley said.

"I assume you're talking to me," Cora said. "Of course, I've been wrong before. It's amazing how wrong someone can be."

"I don't understand," Crowley said. "You mean you just showed up?"

"You weren't answering your phone. Not that I called, by the way. I know you never answer. And I had to get in touch with you. So I rang the bell. I had no idea someone else would buzz me in."

"I didn't buzz her in," Stephanie protested. "I know better than that. I went down to see who it was. Of course I recognized her. It's not like I let in some stranger off the street."

From the look on his face, Crowley might have preferred some stranger off the street. "Oh, of course, of course," he said, clearly fighting for time. "And you invited her in?"

"Someone's dead," Stephanie said.

"Hank Wells," Cora said. "The alleged philandering husband, now the alleged corpse. Who may or may not have blown himself up with a car bomb."

"What?"

Cora gave Crowley a rundown of the situation. He latched on

to it like a drowning man to a life raft, retreating from the social situation to his field of expertise. "This is the guy you were investigating?"

"That's right."

"You start investigating him and he blows up?"

"I don't think it's cause and effect."

"Most things are. And *why* did you feel the need to tell me this?"

"It's not me. Chief Harper's been trying to reach you all day. He wants to check out the girlfriend, and he doesn't have time. He was hoping you'd talk to her."

"Why didn't you do it?"

"I didn't want to."

"Really? That's usually right up your street."

"I was personally involved. Before the incident."

"That's not a deal breaker."

"You wanna argue with me? I didn't want to do it." Cora said to Stephanie, "Some men don't hear women when they tell them they don't want to do something. It's the theory on which date rapes are prosecuted."

"I've heard that," Stephanie said.

Crowley exhaled. "Fine. You want me to talk to the woman, I'll talk to her. Come on. Let's go."

"You want me to go with you?" Cora said.

"Well, I'm not leaving you girls here together. God knows what you'd be plotting."

Chapter

3 6

Crowley drove uptown in silence. Cora studied his profile and wondered how long it would take him to crack. She soon grew tired of the exercise. He was a policeman; he could probably hold out forever.

"Well, you want to talk about it?" Cora said.

"Talk about what?"

"The skinny, straw-haired elephant in the room."

"I'll tell her you said so."

"You were with me just the other day."

"What's your point? We live in other towns. Our relationship's on hiatus. I shouldn't have other friends?"

"This is a particular friend."

"Damn right she is. And a good one, too. She's always been there for me. I've always been there for her. We have each other's backs. I've known her all my life. I met you just last year. She lives in town and we have things in common."

"Apparently, she and I do, too."

"Ouch."

"Is that all you have to say?"

"Well, if you're going to beat me up."

"Oh, is that what I'm doing?"

"Come on, Cora. I've told Stephanie all about you."

"That's nice. Funny you never told me all about her."

"I didn't think you'd be interested."

"Maybe you thought I'd be too interested."

Crowley said nothing, cut off a bus.

"You know you've been accelerating ever since the conversation started. Any faster you'd have to turn on your siren."

Crowley sped down Madeline Greer's block and screeched to a stop in front of her building. "Okay. Let's go."

"I'm not going in," Cora said.

"Don't you want to hear what she has to say?"

"Yeah, but I don't want to be there when she says it. I don't want to muddy the water. I followed the guy here. I may have to testify to that. I don't wanna have to also testify that I questioned the witness."

"Suit yourself," Crowley said. He left Cora in the car, rang the bell, spoke on the intercom. Whatever he said worked. The door was buzzed open and he went up.

He was gone long enough that Cora was beginning to wonder if he was afraid to come back. Then the door opened and he slid into the front seat. "Well, that was interesting," he said.

There was a pause.

Cora said, "You gonna make me ask, or you gonna tell me what?"

"She claims she's not his girlfriend."

"Of course she's going to deny it. The guy's married on the one hand and dead on the other. Not the sort of relationship you wanna claim."

"Maybe not, but I believed her. I'm a cop, and I'm good at these things. I'd say she was telling the truth. According to her, she barely knew the guy. He was just trying to sell her insurance."

"Yeah, right," Cora scoffed. "And you fell for that?"

"I took note of her claim. In my opinion, it has validity." Crowley cocked his head. "Now here's the interesting part. According to her, a couple of days ago somebody came around trying to shake her down for sleeping with a married man. She told him he was all wet, but he just laughed and demanded money. As soon as he left she called Hank demanding to know what the hell was going on. He came rushing over and tried to calm her down. The guy'd made a mistake, but he'd handle it. Just leave it to him. There was nothing to worry about.

"While he was trying to convince her the guy came back, and tried to blackmail him. She said he stalled the guy off for forty-eight hours."

"You believed her?"

"Oh, I believed her. You tried to get me to blackmail the guy and I turned you down. Who'd you get to pinch-hit?"

"You're making a lot of assumptions."

"I'm making *one* assumption. It's one a child of three could make. You wanna fess up now, or you wanna keep playing games?"

"I prefer games."

"I'm sure you do. It now occurs to me you were mighty reluctant to go upstairs. Maybe you didn't want to be recognized. Could it be the pinch hitter was you?"

"Come on, Crowley. She said it was a guy. You think I was mistaken for a guy? That's not very flattering."

"Of course not. But you might have told her to *say* it was a guy."

Cora rattled her fingers alongside her head. "Doublethink. What have you got, snakes in your head? 'Hi, I'm Cora Felton the Puzzle Lady and I'm going to blackmail you now, but if the police ask you about it would you please tell them it was a man that did it?' Have fun trying to sell that one."

"Fine. You didn't do it yourself. But you had it done."

"Prove it."

"I don't have to prove it. I'll just tell Harper you did it and he can take it from there."

Cora took a breath. "Okay, let's calm down for a minute. I caught you with your girlfriend and you're taking it out on me." When Crowley started to protest she said, "Quite understandable. When you've been married as many times as I have, you get used to men's behavior. The counteroffensive is a simple and effective ploy. I get that. Let's drop it and move on."

"Wait a minute, wait minute," Crowley said. "This is not a ploy. Blackmail is a crime."

"So is murder. Could we concentrate on the big picture here? What's important is what this woman did, not what I did. The two have nothing to do with each other."

"Funny you should say that."

Cora looked at him suspiciously. "Why?"

"Oh. You and the woman having nothing to do with each other. No connection whatsoever."

"What's funny about that?"

Crowley reached in his pocket, pulled out a piece of paper. "She gave me this."

Cora reached for it.

"I'd prefer you didn't get your fingerprints on it," Crowley said.

"*You're* touching it."

"By the edges. And I touched it when she handed it to me. Not knowing what it was."

"What is it?"

Crowley turned the paper around.

It was a crossword puzzle.

Puzzled Indemnity

Across

1 Creature in the movie "Blackfish"
5 *Column down
9 Spiced tea drink
13 Terrier type
15 Celestial bear
16 Skipper's spot
17 *Number of numbers
18 Start of a message
20 Fashion designer whose birth name is Isaacs
22 Garlicky sauces
23 Toon Chihuahua
24 *Type of wood
25 More of the message
31 Batik artists
35 Company formed by the Sperry-Burroughs merger
36 Rugrats
38 Punster's skill

39 Prey for owls
40 On __ (busy)
42 Trig function
43 Wolfed down
44 Winter coating
45 Sudden fall
47 Far from genial
49 More of the message
51 Eustachian tube site
53 Course figure
54 *Position
57 *Venue
61 End of the message
63 Out-and-out
65 Invent, as a word
66 "Yeah, sure!"
67 Showy violet
68 Drops the curtain on
69 Ellipsis trio
70 After the bell

Down

1 United Nations Day mo.
2 Fan shouts
3 Newspaper sales: Abbr.
4 Word with Bay or gray
5 Really ticked off
6 "... __ quit!" (ultimatum ender)
7 Jimmy Carter's sch.
8 XM __
9 Like a well-used blackboard eraser
10 Prefix with sphere

11 Brewpub offerings
12 Online exchanges, briefly
14 Close at hand
19 Prods into action
21 Takes care of
25 Capable of mistakes
26 Author Loos
27 Smoking, gambling, etc., to some
28 Language suffix
29 In __ (unborn)
30 Yuletide quaff
32 "Dallas" surname
33 One of the Fab Four
34 Dutch painter Jan
37 Partner of tails
41 Barn-dance seating
42 Source of green energy
44 Big name in hotels
46 Thrash but good
48 Mortise mates
50 Underdogs' wins
52 Gave a makeover to
54 "Follow me!"
55 Blyton or Bagnold
56 __-call (pre-Election-Day message, maybe)
58 Footnote abbr.
59 Sicilian peak
60 Lab procedure
61 Mixologist's "rocks"
62 Bring home
64 Deli loaf

Cora's eyes bugged out of her head. "You've got to be kidding me!"

"I'm not."

"Where did this come from?"

"I told you. The woman gave it to me. She found it under her door."

"So she gave it to you?"

"Well, she wasn't going to, but I asked her if anything peculiar had happened lately."

"And she whipped out a crossword puzzle?" Cora said sarcastically.

"Actually, she mentioned the blackmail. Which would have been my first choice. But I'm a cop. Just because I get an answer doesn't mean I stop asking the question. I asked her if she'd heard from the blackmailer again; she said she hadn't. I asked her if there'd been a note; she said there wasn't. I asked her if anything else peculiar had happened; she said yes, but it wasn't a note. And she gave me this." Crowley looked at her. "Now, if you've used up all your arguments for why she shouldn't have got it or why she shouldn't have given it to me, you wannna discuss the puzzle itself?"

"You know I can't solve it."

"I'm not talking about solving it. Why do you think she got it?"

"I have no idea."

"Me neither. But it certainly cements your connection to this woman."

"Maybe that's the point."

"How can that be the point?"

"I don't know, but you start making assumptions. I'm going to make some, too."

"Fine. You wanna make something about this?"

Crowley pulled out a sudoku.

6					8			
4		3						
9	7	2			3	6		
7	6							
2				6				
			4	8			5	
	4		3		7			9
	9	7	1		4		6	8
			5			1		7

Cora gawked. "Are you kidding me?"

"No, but it's something connected to you. And it's something you can solve."

"So what? It's just numbers. Without the crossword puzzle it's not going to tell you anything."

"No, we'll have to solve that, too."

"Be my guest."

"I'm no better at crosswords than you are."

"Right. So run it down to your boys at the station."

"They've gone home."

"What are you telling me? We've gotta go all the way to Baker-haven and have my niece solve it?"

"No. I happen to know someone who's good at crossword puzzles."

"You do? Well, why didn't you say so? We can—" Cora's eyes widened. "Oh, no!"

"She does the *New York Times* puzzle every day."

"Even Saturday?"

"Yeah."

"I hate her."

"I know."

"Come on. Saturday's hard."

"How would *you* know?"

"Sherry told me. You are *not* having your girlfriend solve this puzzle."

"She's not my girlfriend."

"I don't care what you call her. It's not happening."

"You don't have to be there."

"What do you mean, I don't have to be there? Of course I have to be there."

"I can call Chief Harper tomorrow, say you got ahold of me, I interviewed the woman, got these puzzles, and got 'em solved."

"How about the sudoku?"

"She can do sudoku."

"Of course she can. Well, she's not going to do it. You left with me. You come back with a crossword puzzle, she's going to know I couldn't solve it."

"Actually . . ."

Cora's eyes blazed. "You told her I couldn't do puzzles!"

"In strictest confidence."

Cora told Crowley what she thought of his strictest confidence, what she thought of Stephanie, what she thought of crossword puzzles, and what she thought of him, though not necessarily in that order. Her language was colorful, if not downright actionable. In mid-tirade, without missing a beat, Cora demanded, "Well, what are you waiting for? Let's go!"

Cora was torn between wanting Stephanie to solve the cross-word puzzle and wanting to strangle her for being able to do so. Cora had solved the sudoku in the car on the way there, leaving her with nothing to do. She paced up and down Crowley's living room in smoldering frustration.

"It's not enough you have to torture me with an old girlfriend, you gotta humiliate me by telling her my failings."

"It's not a failing," Stephanie said. "It's a skill you don't have."

"Wanna see a skill I *do* have?"

Stephanie smiled. "Believe me, I wasn't taunting."

"Don't be nice," Cora said. "It's harder if you're nice."

Crowley exhaled noisily.

Without looking up from the paper Stephanie said, "You expected some huge revelation?"

"Why?"

"It looks like a pretty tame message."

"What is it?"

"Hang on. I'm not done."

"I thought you knew the message."

"I do," Stephanie said. "It's 'Hang on, I'm not done.' The message is, 'Mind games have begun. You hang on. I'm not done.'"

"What the hell does that mean?" Crowley said.

"I have no idea."

"Cora?"

"Who, me? I thought I was just a spectator."

"Don't be silly. Other people solve the puzzle. You're the one who figures out what it means."

"What's to figure out? Our killer has suggested that more murders are in the offing. Fine. We'll be on our guard. Not that we weren't already."

"Forewarned is forearmed," Crowley said.

"Yeah," Cora said. "An octopus is forewarned twice."

Crowley stared at her, but Stephanie burst out laughing. "You're actually very good with words."

"Just as long as they don't intersect," Cora said.

"Oh," Crowley said, finally getting it. "But aside from that, the puzzle doesn't mean anything?"

"No, and that's not all. It doesn't reference the sudoku."

"Should it?" Stephanie said.

"It came with the sudoku. They can't be unrelated. Without the crossword the sudoku's just numbers. There should be something in the crossword that tells us why the sudoku is there."

"Wait a minute," Stephanie said. "You think these are puzzles the killer sent to the victim's girlfriend?"

"That's right," Cora said.

"Why?"

"I don't know why, but they usually are."

"Usually? How many killers make up crossword puzzles?"

"More than you'd think," Cora said. "Accepting that absurd premise as a given, the question is how does the crossword relate to the sudoku and how do both puzzles relate to the crime?"

"You may be in luck," Stephanie said.

"What do you mean?"

"Some of these clues are starred."

"Well, why didn't you say so?"

"You went off on a crossword killer rant." Cora opened her mouth, and Stephanie put up her hand. "No offense meant."

"What are the clues?"

"Here. Look."

O	R	C	A		F	O	U	R		C	H	A	I
C	A	I	R	N	U	R	S	A		H	E	L	M
T	H	R	E	E	M	I	N	D	G	A	M	E	S
	S	C	A	A	S	I		A	I	O	L	I	S
			R	E	N			O	A	K			
H	A	V	E	B	E	G	U	N		D	Y	E	R	S
U	N	I	S	Y	S		T	O	T	S		W	I	T
M	I	C	E		T	H	E	G	O		S	I	N	E
A	T	E		H	O	A	R		P	L	U	N	G	E
N	A	S	T	Y		Y	O	U	H	A	N	G	O	N
		E	A	R		P	A	R					
C	E	N	T	E	R		S	T	R	E	E	T	
I	M	N	O	T	D	O	N	E		U	T	T	E	R
C	O	I	N		I	B	E	T		P	A	N	S	Y
E	N	D	S		D	O	T	S		L	A	T	E

Stephanie held out the puzzle and pointed. "5 across: column down—four. 17 across: number of numbers—three. 24 across: type of wood—oak. 54 across: position—center. 57 across: venue—street."

"Oak Street!" Cora said. "And the numbers will give us the address."

Stephanie snatched up the sudoku.

6	1	5	2	7	9	8	3	4
4	8	3	6	1	5	9	7	2
9	7	2	8	4	3	6	1	5
7	6	4	5	9	1	2	8	3
2	5	8	7	3	6	4	9	1
1	3	9	4	8	2	7	5	6
8	4	1	3	6	7	5	2	9
5	9	7	1	2	4	3	6	8
3	2	6	9	5	8	1	4	7

"Fourth column down, three center numbers are: five, seven, four. There you go. Five-seventy-four Oak Street."

"I'm a New York girl born and bred," Cora said. "You don't have to tell me there's no Oak Street in New York City."

"That's for sure," Crowley said.

"But there is in Bakerhaven."

"Okay. Whose address is it?"

"I have no idea. I could call Chief Harper, but he'll want to hear the whole story and I'll be on the phone for hours."

"Why bother?" Stephanie said. "We can look it up on Map-Quest."

"Yeah, but Sergeant Stone Age doesn't have a computer. Surely you know that."

Stephanie dug in her purse, whipped out an iPhone, began tapping the screen. "What's the address we want? Ah, yes. Five-seventy-four Oak Street. Bakerhaven." She punched it in. "Oh."

"What is it?" Cora asked.

Stephanie held it up for her to see.

Cora's mouth fell open.

"Well? Whose address is it?" Crowley said.

"Hank Wells'."

Chief Harper looked like a man on the verge of a violent eruption or a nervous breakdown. Cora figured it was touch and go.

Harper pointed to the crossword lying on his desk, looked at Sergeant Crowley. "The woman gave you this?"

"That's right."

"And she told you she was being blackmailed over an affair she *wasn't* having with the decedent. And did the blackmailer by any chance leave this puzzle?"

"According to her, it was slipped under her door."

"How soon after the blackmailer left?"

"She didn't say."

"You didn't ask?"

"It's your theory, Chief. With the benefit of hindsight."

"Hindsight?"

"Yeah. The puzzle's solved, and there seems to be some connection."

"Yeah. To the guy she wasn't having an affair with." Harper turned to Cora. "You have any idea what that means?"

"I haven't a clue."

Harper jerked his thumb. "And you needed your lawyer here to help you say that?"

Becky had insisted on coming along when she heard what Crowley would be telling Chief Harper.

"I don't think I need a lawyer, Chief, but Becky needs the work."

"Why? She hasn't got time for the work she has now."

"I beg your pardon?" Becky said.

"You were supposed to produce your client's life insurance policy."

"I don't see why you need it."

"If her husband really was planning on killing her for the money, it would be motivation to beat him to the punch."

Becky smiled. "Are you suggesting she plead self-defense?"

"I'm suggesting you produce the document you promised to produce two days ago. Or have you changed your mind?"

"My client's looking for it, Chief. If she can't find it, we may have to start inquiring of insurance companies."

"She doesn't know which one?"

"The amount was the thing that grabbed her attention. However, if you've ever met my client, I think you'd agree it's very unlikely she constructed a crossword puzzle giving her own address."

"This is all very nice," Crowley said, "but New York's a big city, and I happen to have cases of my own. If we could speed this along."

"Anything you haven't told me about the girlfriend?"

"She claims not to be the girlfriend."

"I take that with a grain of salt."

"I'm not so sure."

"Right. It's not your case, so you don't mind complicating it. If you were in charge, how'd she look to you?"

Crowley frowned, considered. "Too good to be true. I wouldn't write her off."

"There you are."

"And her blackmail story?"

"Could be a complete fabrication. Just like her claiming she's not the woman."

"You think that's likely?"

"No. *You* do. I think she's *not* the woman and her blackmail story's true. But you're talking gut reaction with no investigation whatsoever. I'm a New York cop. I can't drop everything I'm doing to investigate a Bakerhaven homicide."

"I understand."

"So is there anything else I can tell you about the woman?"

"If you *were* investigating her, what would you do next?"

"Well, I'd sit her down with a sketch artist, try to get a picture of the blackmailer. That's one thing I could do for you. You probably don't have a police sketch artist."

"He's on vacation," Harper deadpanned. "Thanks. I appreciate it."

"I'll put someone on it." Crowley got up. "Okay, I gotta be going."

"I'll walk you out," Cora said.

The minute Cora and Crowley were outside, she wheeled on him. "All right, what was that all about?"

"What was what all about?"

"You're going to make him a police sketch of the blackmailer?"

"Why? You afraid it might be someone you know?"

"Don't be an ass."

"Oh? You have someone blackmail the woman, use me as a cat's-paw to interview her, lie to me about your involvement, and *I'm* being an ass?"

"If you know all of that and then act as if you didn't so you can turn on me and make that accusation, you're being an ass."

Crowley blinked. "I'm not sure I even follow that. But when you sort it all out, I'm not sure I'm in the wrong."

"If you deceived me, you're in the wrong."

"So. It all comes back to Stephanie."

"I wasn't talking about Stephanie."

"Really? You could have fooled me." Crowley got in the car,

slammed the door. He rolled down the window. "You know, I could help you a lot more if you'd just level with me. Good luck with your case. Hope it doesn't come back to bite you." He slammed the car into gear. "I'll try to get you a bad sketch artist," he said, and drove off.

Chapter

"What a mess!" Cora stalked Becky's office like a caged tiger. "What a mess!" she repeated, adding a few choice modifiers.

"It's not so bad," Becky said.

"It's not so bad for *you*. You got a client paying you money and no one's charging you with blackmail."

"You're not guilty of blackmail."

"Wonderful. That's the sort of thing you like to hear your lawyer say."

Cora marched to the window, flung it open.

"If you're thinking of jumping, it's only one floor."

A blast of cold air hit Cora in the face. She closed the window, turned around. "I could probably beat this blackmail rap. I got a hell of a lawyer. On the other hand, I got a puzzle I can't even begin to figure out. Why the hell does a New York woman who may or may not have been sleeping with a philandering husband who may or may not be dead wind up with a crossword puzzle yielding the possible corpse's address?"

"You fault yourself for not being able to figure that out?"

"I fault myself for not having a clue. Here's a crime that doesn't make any sense. There's a million-dollar insurance policy, but the wrong person's dead. The mistress isn't the mistress, but she seems to have some connection with the victim."

"She's more connected against than connecting," Becky said. "Unless she sent herself that puzzle."

"You're in an awful good mood."

"Well, why shouldn't I be? Things are popping very nicely for me. My client's got a perfect alibi and no motive. And she's so scatterbrained I'm going to rack up a bunch of billable hours tracking down who issued her policy."

"Come on, Becky. You know you won't rest easy until you know who did it."

"I'd *like* to know who did it, but I don't *have* to."

"Yeah, well, I do," Cora said. She picked up her purse, fidgeted, set it down, paced back to the window.

"Would you sit down?" Becky said. "You're driving me crazy."

"*I'm* driving *you* crazy? I thought you were the one without a care in the world." Cora flopped into the client's chair. Snorted. "Crowley's got a girlfriend."

"Oh?" Becky said.

"A peace/love hippie who's never gotten out of the sixties."

"Isn't that your gig?" Becky said.

"I was never a hippie. I did try to levitate the Pentagon."

"How'd that work for you?"

"It failed to live up to expectations. Kind of a metaphor for life." Cora bounced up, resumed pacing. "Anyway, he's known Stephanie—that's her name—he's known Stephanie ever since they were old enough to reach each other's laps. I gather he was seeing her the whole time he was seeing me."

Becky whistled. "And you wonder why you can't concentrate on the murder."

"I don't wonder. I'm just not happy about it. And that's not all.

Crowley had to go and tell her I can't solve crossword puzzles. You know who solved the one we brought in? And she's *good* at it. Not Sherry-caliber good, but good. She does the Saturday *Times* puzzle."

"What about Sunday?"

"Sunday's just bigger. Saturday's actually harder. And you know the worst part of it?" Cora said.

"What's that?"

"I *like* her," Cora said disgustedly. "She's *nice*! Ain't that a kick in the head? I can't even resent her without feeling guilty about it. I've *always* hated the other woman. It's one of the perks of the relationship. Having some cheap slut to disparage. But *no*! Little Miss Hippie Britches has to deny me that."

"Hippie Britches?"

"See? I can't even come up with a good derogatory nickname. As if that weren't bad enough, I feel guilty about Melvin."

Becky's eyes widened. "You slept with Melvin!"

Cora waved it away. "No. Perish the thought. But when Crowley wouldn't blackmail the woman, I had Melvin do it. Wouldn't you say that was subconsciously cheating on him?"

"No, I wouldn't say that, because I wouldn't think that. You needed a blackmailer, and Melvin's typecast for the role."

"Yeah, I know," Cora said. She flopped back into the chair, picked up her purse, set it down.

"Good God, will you stop fidgeting! You're driving me crazy and—" Becky's mouth fell open. "Oh, my God!"

"What?"

"You stopped smoking!"

Cora glared at her.

"What were you doing?" Becky said. "Waiting to see how long it would take me to notice?"

"Frankly, I wasn't thinking of you at all."

"Why didn't you tell me you quit smoking?"

"I didn't want to talk about it. I *still* don't want to talk about it."

"How long has it been?"

Cora said nothing.

"I haven't seen you smoke since this case started. Three, four days. I bet it's been a week."

"Nine days," Cora said.

"That's terrific!"

"Easy for you to say. You don't smoke."

"You on a patch?"

"No."

"Chew the Nicorette gum?"

"That's like kissing your brother."

"Kissing your brother?"

"You get all the nicotine with none of the pleasure."

"You used to kiss your brother?"

"I never had a brother. Look, I'm bouncing off the walls a little, so maybe I'm missing something. If so, I'd sure like you to tell me what it is."

Brittany burst in the door. "Got it!" she cried triumphantly, waving a document. "It was in the one place I never thought to look."

"Where's that?" Becky said.

"In his file cabinet."

"His file cabinet?"

"Yes. But it wasn't in the file marked IMPORTANT PAPERS."

"Where was it?"

"In the file marked LIFE INSURANCE."

Cora rolled her eyes. "And you just found it now?"

"Well, I wasn't looking for a file marked LIFE INSURANCE. If he was trying to hide the policy, why would he leave it there?"

"I guess he wasn't trying to hide the policy," Cora said.

"Of course he was trying to hide the policy," Brittany said. "Otherwise I would have found it."

Becky jumped in before Cora could formulate some devastatingly sarcastic put-down. "Well, I'm glad you found it. Even if Harper does think it's a motive for murder."

"Why is that a motive for murder?"

"Your husband was trying to kill you, and you beat him to the punch."

"That's silly."

"Of course it is, and I'll have no problem proving it. At least this will get him off my back."

The phone rang. Becky scooped it up. "Becky Baldwin. . . . Hi, Chief. . . . No, I haven't forgotten. She just found it. She's here right now. . . . No, I'm not stalling. She just got here. I'll bring it over."

Becky hung up the phone. "See what I mean? All right, let's take a look at the policy, make sure it says what you think it does."

Becky skimmed the document. Turned the page. "Here it is. Double-indemnity clause. One million dollars. Everything seems to be in order and—" Becky's face froze.

Brittany looked alarmed. "What's the matter? Isn't it for a million dollars?"

"Yes, it is. One million dollars, two million for accidental death."

"So what's the problem?"

"You're the *beneficiary*. It's not a million dollars on *you*. It's a million dollars on *him*!"

"Widow charged!" Rick Reed proclaimed from the front steps of the Bakerhaven police station. "In a stunning development in the firebombing death of Bakerhaven resident Hank Wells, the grieving widow has been arrested and charged with his murder. Chief Harper refused to comment on the incident, but high-placed sources indicate that new evidence has come to light linking Brittany Wells with the crime. Late this afternoon rumors surfaced of a million-dollar double-indemnity life insurance policy on the victim, Hank Wells, giving the widow, Brittany Wells, a two-million-dollar motive for wanting him dead. Becky Baldwin, Brittany's hotshot young attorney, could not be reached for comment."

Sherry picked up the remote control from the coffee table, froze Rick Reed with his head cocked and his mouth wide open.

Jennifer pointed at the screen and squealed delightedly.

"*Becky Baldwin* could not be reached for comment?" Sherry said. "When did Becky Baldwin ever pass up a chance to strut her stuff on television?"

Aaron grinned. "Strut her stuff?"

"Becky didn't trust herself to go on TV," Cora said. "She wasn't sure she could answer questions without looking like she wanted to strangle her client."

"Why?"

"Are you kidding me? The idiot hired her to find out if her husband was trying to kill her because he took out a double-indemnity life insurance policy, only the policy was on *him*. How stupid do you have to be to miss *that* little tidbit?"

"Is she really that dumb?" Sherry said.

"Jennifer could outwit her."

"So what? Jennifer outwits me," Aaron said.

Jennifer squealed at being mentioned.

"Trust me, she's a tree stump. Either that or she's the most cunning criminal mastermind ever. And she's not. The woman's just plain stupid. No, Becky's better off standing pat and waiting for Chief Harper to come down to earth. He was so thrilled with the motive he picked her up without stopping to think it over. When he wakes up he's gonna realize she was in his office when it happened and couldn't have set the damn thing off."

"Yeah, but if it was a car bomb that went off when he started the car—"

"He was in the passenger seat," Cora said impatiently. "Everything points to the fact he was trying to kill her. If the names on the policy were reversed, it would all make perfect sense."

"Maybe there's another policy," Aaron said.

"Not according to Hartford Life."

"Couldn't he have taken out a policy with another company?"

"He certainly could. And Becky may spend a ton of her client's money having me look for it. But she doesn't have to. Chief Harper's got motive. Or he thinks he does. He's still gotta prove she knew the policy existed. It's not going to be easy. But even if he could, he hasn't got the opportunity, he hasn't got the means, and he hasn't even got a positive ID on the corpse. Which is why he let her go."

"He let her go?" Sherry said.

"Rick Reed missed that tidbit. Only one of many factual errors in his report."

"Such as?"

"Start with the lead. Widow charged. She wasn't charged with anything. She was picked up for questioning. You can call that being arrested—she was read her Miranda rights. She exercised her right to an attorney, which didn't take much doing since Becky was right there. She wouldn't let her answer questions and said charge her or release her. So they called in Henry Firth."

"The prosecutor was there?" Sherry said. "I don't recall that from Rick's report."

"Probably because it spoils his story," Aaron said. "The whole widow-charged bit."

"And he let her go?"

"Ratface ran out of steam when he found out Chief Harper was her alibi witness."

"You've gotta stop calling him Ratface," Sherry said. "You're going to slip and do it at the wrong time."

"Ratface!" Jennifer cried gleefully.

"Or that'll happen."

"Ratface!"

"See what you started."

"Me?" Cora said. "I didn't do anything. She got excited because Mommy said it."

"Right, right," Sherry said. "You make up the expression and I'm the bad guy."

Cora picked up the zapper, clicked Play. Rick Reed unfroze and finished the story. He talked for about three minutes and divulged no new information whatsoever.

Cora zapped the screen again, said to Aaron, "So, what's the paper going to run?"

"The boring, factual version of the story. The widow was brought in for questioning and released; both the police and her attorney declined to comment."

"Sell a lot of papers?"

"No, but I can sleep at night."

"I'm sure Rick can, too. He's blissfully unaware he's doing anything wrong."

"Yeah," Aaron said. "You know the difference between a journalist and a gossip columnist?"

"No."

"Neither does Rick. He reports rumors and innuendo. If I don't have a source, I don't have a story."

"Your man has integrity," Cora told Sherry. "Did you know that when you married him?"

"Why? Is that bad?"

"I don't know. I never married one."

"Speaking of sources," Aaron said.

"Yeah?"

"You got anything you haven't shared yet would send me running back to the paper?"

"Relating to the men I've married? I certainly do, but you're not going to get it."

"You're in a much better mood," Sherry said.

"I am *not* in a much better mood," Cora said. "I'm punchy. I'm losing it. I might say anything. It's a good thing I didn't have to deal with Henry Firth."

"Ratface!"

Cora got up, let Buddy out, let him in again, threw a bowl of kibble on the floor, and went back to sleep.

The phone rang at ten thirty-five. She fumbled the receiver to her ear, murmured, "Mumph."

"Wake up. I need you."

"Becky?"

"Yeah. Get in here."

"What's up?"

"You see Rick Reed's report?"

"His fairy tale?"

"It just came true."

Cora splashed water on her face, struggled into her clothes. Her skirt was tight. Of course it was. She hadn't dared step on the scales since she stopped smoking. If he skirt was tight after ten days, what would it be like in a month?

Cora went out the door, slipped on a patch of ice. She regained her balance, cursed the gods of just about everything, got in her car, and sped to town a little too fast for road conditions.

Becky was at her desk, talking on the phone. "How large a device are we talking? . . . Could it fit in the palm of my hand? . . . Well, could I carry it in my purse, surreptitiously reach in, and press it? . . . That's the wrong answer. Thanks anyway." She hung up.

"What's going on?" Cora said.

"Motive and opportunity just fell into the prosecutor's lap. An expert technician from the bomb squad managed to recover enough of the explosive device to determine it wasn't any ordinary car bomb. It wasn't wired into the ignition to go off when the car started. It had a radio trigger detonated by remote control."

"They're claiming she set it off while she was in the police station?"

Becky spread her arms. "Perfect alibi."

"Yes, but how would she know he was in the car?"

"That's what I'll have to argue. Doesn't matter. The fact is it wasn't physically possible. Now it is. And if I raise the point, it will mean we've gone to trial. Do you know how far that is from yesterday's we-haven't-enough-grounds-to-hold-her-on-suspicion-of-murder?"

"Where is she?"

"She's being booked and fingerprinted. They're arraigning her at noon."

"For the murder of whom? They haven't IDed the corpse."

Becky grimaced. "That's the other kick in the head. They got the dental records. It's a match. The grieving widow is officially a widow. The man she's charged with killing is on the policy she worked so hard to find. You couldn't ask for a worse case to defend. If I don't put her on the stand, she's dead meat. If I do put her on the stand, she's such a nitwit the prosecutor could probably get her to confess to the Lindbergh kidnapping."

"You're too young to cite Charles Lindbergh."

"I went to school."

"Whaddya want me to do?"

"I don't know. The facts of the case are terrible. I'd like them to disappear. Failing that, I'd like some new facts that contradict these facts, or at least cast reasonable doubt."

"Where do you want me to start?"

"Ordinarily, I'd say the girlfriend. If only you hadn't blackmailed her."

"Are we going to keep coming back to that?"

"I certainly hope not. How about it? You got another angle?"

"There's the firebug."

"No, there isn't. Chief Harper didn't bite, and he was plenty pissed you finessed Rick Reed into asking him about it. You know and I know the guy had nothing to do with it, so lay off."

"Getting a conscience? I thought you were a lawyer."

"I'm a good lawyer. I don't waste time beating a dead horse."

"Well, you woke me up and got me in here. Whaddya want?"

"Oh," Becky said. "Did I just want someone to listen to me gripe? I hope not. That would mean I was really losing it."

"Becky."

"I want you with me in case they throw anything at me at the arraignment."

"What could they possibly throw at you at the arraignment?'

"I have no idea. But I'm spooked. Things come in threes. We have the detonator and the dentist. What else starting with *D* could possibly go wrong?"

"The detective?" Cora said.

"Bite your tongue."

Judge Hobbs surveyed the crowded courtroom with displeasure. Cora suppressed a smile. She knew how he felt. This was a simple arraignment, and it was threatening to become a media circus. Rick Reed and his camera crew were set up in the back of the courtroom to film the event, and that was only because they had been denied permission to set up closer.

Brittany Wells was escorted into the courtroom by Dan Finley, the least threatening police presence imaginable. Dan was doing everything in his power to reassure her. She was not in handcuffs, and he was treating her as solicitously as if she were his date for the policeman's ball. He led her to the defense table, installed her next to Becky Baldwin, and withdrew to a discreet distance.

Judge Hobbs called court to order and addressed the prosecutor. "Mr. Firth, with what is the defendant charged?"

"Murder, Your Honor, in the death of her husband, Hank Wells."

"Miss Baldwin, how does your client plead?"

"Not guilty, Your Honor."

"Very well. A plea of not guilty is entered and the defendant is bound over for trial."

"Your Honor, I would request reasonable bail," Becky said.

Henry Firth nearly gagged. "Bail? How can she request bail? The defendant profited from her crime to the tune of two million dollars. If ever there was a reason to jump bail, I would think that's it."

Becky smiled. "She doesn't have it, Your Honor. And from the noises coming from the insurance company, I doubt if she'll have it anytime soon."

Henry Firth's nose twitched. "That's silly."

"I quite agree. And I'll be sure to quote you to the insurance company. You want to testify if they start making trouble?"

"Yes, isn't that clever," Henry Firth said. "The fact that the defendant doesn't profit from her crime as quickly as she had hoped in no way reflects on the validity of the motive. Even if she never gets it, the fact is she thought she would. This is a cold-blooded murder for profit. The idea of bail is outrageous."

"Personally, I think binding her over for trial is outrageous," Becky said, "given that you have no evidence against her beyond the money you *claim* she mistakenly hoped to obtain. I would say the defense is making a large concession not contesting the arraignment."

Judge Hobbs banged the gavel. "I would say that no one is conceding anything. You're like a bunch of schoolchildren bragging about who's smarter."

"Oh, Your Honor—" Henry Firth said.

"Aside from the insurance money she's not getting," Becky said, "she has no other assets. She's not going to run away from the insurance money any more than she's going to run away from whatever bail you force her to raise."

"I would tend to agree," Judge Hobbs said. "Mr. Prosecutor, can you think of any extenuating circumstance that would make this particular defendant a flight risk?"

Henry Firth cleared his throat. "Murder is a serious charge, Your Honor."

"I don't need a lecture on the law. Murder is always a serious charge. The only question here is how much money will it take to encourage the defendant to show up and face it." Judge Hobbs considered. "Bail is set at a hundred thousand dollars."

"Oh, Your Honor," Henry Firth protested. "That's only a ten-thousand-dollar bond."

"I can do the math. Bail is set at a hundred thousand dollars; defendant is remanded to custody until such time as bail is raised."

"What do you want me to do?" Cora said.

Becky considered. "I have no idea. Short of getting someone to confess, I don't know what I need. I got a woman arraigned on the skimpiest of evidence. As soon as Henry Firth wakes up, he's going to realize it, too. My best bet is to just stall things along, let him try to make a case."

"Is your client happy with that strategy?"

"I don't think she's competent to make that determination. It would mean understanding the facts, evaluating them, and placing them in the larger context of the situation. I've been to law school, and I have a fairly good grasp on what's happening. She hasn't and she doesn't."

"But she's willing to let you act in her behalf?"

"That's right. And as long as I'm in that position, I will continue to make decisions in her best interest in spite of her."

"At the moment it's in her best interest to sit tight?"

"Yeah."

"So what's the problem?"

Becky made a face. "The problem is until this matter is settled the insurance company isn't going to pay off. Brittany's liquid assets are now tied up in a bail bond. Leaving her no money for retainers and legal fees."

"I'm not getting paid?" Cora said.

"Maybe not as quickly as you'd hoped, but trust me you'll get paid. I just may need to cut back on your services."

"You're firing me?"

"Perish the thought. I'm allowing you to control your own destiny. At the moment, I don't know what to assign you to do. On the other hand, if you can think of anything worth doing, do it. I'll see that you get paid."

"I hate that."

"Why?"

"Are you kidding me? I have to make a value judgment on my every move. As if I didn't have enough trouble concentrating on the case while I'm dying for a cigarette."

"I'm sorry. What would you like me to do?"

"Oh, Becky. Don't lob one across the plate like that. It's so hard to resist."

The door opened and Chief Harper came in.

"Don't you ever knock?" Becky said.

"I thought it was a public office," Harper said.

"It's a *one-room* office. It's a public office *and* a private office. See the problem?"

Chief Harper waved it away. "Yeah, yeah. I've got my own problems."

"What problems?" Cora said. "You're a winner. Your perp just got arraigned."

"You'd think that, wouldn't you?" Chief Harper sighed. "Henry Firth isn't happy."

"When's Ratface ever happy?"

"Please." Harper winced at the nickname. "I shouldn't be spilling trade secrets in front of the defense, but he's not happy about the case."

"You're breaking my heart," Becky said. "What's his problem?"

"He charged this woman without thinking it through. Just because a remote-control device makes it possible this woman killed her husband, it doesn't make it likely. It certainly doesn't prove it beyond a reasonable doubt. The only real indication she killed her husband is she had such a powerful motive."

"You gotta love a good motive," Cora said.

"That's what you'd think. But actually it's kind of a curse. He's prosecuting the woman. The motive's so good he can't dismiss, but the evidence is so sketchy he can't convict. It puts him in a no-win situation, and, wouldn't you know it, he's blaming me."

"So that's why you weren't in court."

"I thought Dan needed the exposure. Anyway, I think Henry's starting to realize the idea she rigged a car bomb is going to be a pretty tough sell."

"That would be my opinion," Becky said. "I'm pleased to hear he shares it."

Harper looked alarmed. "You're not going to quote me on that."

"Relax, Chief. You're among friends," Cora said. "So, to what do we owe the pleasure of your company? You come here just to dump on the prosecutor?"

"That's not what I was doing."

"You could have fooled me. Anyway, the defendant will be delighted to know the case against her is so bad."

"Yeah, yeah," Harper said. "Any time you're through screwing around you might want to take a look at this." He reached in his overcoat pocket, took out a rolled-up manila envelope. "This was delivered to the police station." He pulled out a piece of paper.

It was a crossword puzzle.

Parnell Hall

Across

1 Food pkg. bars
5 Musical partner of Peter and Mary
9 Adjust the lenses
14 Raines or Cinders
15 Italian wine area
16 Be nuts about
17 Start of a message
19 Trace of color
20 Feature of a work boot or pub dart
21 Fiddle around
22 "___ Miz"
23 The Beatles' "___ the Walrus"
24 Doorbell sound
28 More of the message
34 Step down
36 Qatari export
37 Scored 100 on, perhaps
38 Pizazz

39 "The Hobbit" ring-bearer
41 Super review
42 Building wings
43 Lobster trap
44 Dealers in scrap cloth
46 More of the message
49 Jury members, in theory
50 Stooge who parodied Adolf
51 Évian, e.g.
53 City opposite El Paso
57 Eskimos, Navajos et al.
62 Tennyson's Enoch
63 End of the message
64 Studied the stars
65 Object to
66 U.S. rights org.
67 Downhill racers
68 Hippies' homes
69 Come across as

Down

1 Drivers' turnabouts, slangily
2 Whodunit's essence
3 Whodunit element
4 "Ditto!"
5 Paperhanger's need
6 St. Francis's city
7 Lone Star State sch.
8 Travel mug part
9 Daughter of Mohammed
10 Valhalla chief
11 Knock on the noggin
12 Arm-twist
13 Tea-leaves reader
18 Better, to a hip-hopper
21 President before Fillmore
23 Bibliographical "ditto"
24 Angler's basket
25 "__, ball!" (classic Ed Norton line)
26 __-Turkish War of 1911-12
27 Capital of Belarus
29 Gear part
30 Blue-haired Simpson
31 "Veni," translated
32 Prying tool
33 Shangri-las
35 First six letters of a standard eye chart
40 Investment firm T. __ Price
45 In pieces
47 Modifies, as a law
48 Donny or Marie
52 Hangs in the balance
53 Pricey British cars, for short
54 River to the Caspian Sea
55 Wood-shaping tool
56 Swamp growth
57 Region on a Risk game board
58 Tax-deferred plans
59 French Riviera city
60 Earnhardt or Earnhardt Jr.
61 Blighted area
63 Dennis the Menace, e.g.

"What the hell?" Cora said.

"It was slipped under the front door, actually. No one noticed. Dan was at the arraignment; I was in my office. Dan found it when he got back."

"I'll be damned."

Harper held it out to Cora. "It's a photocopy, so you can solve it."

Cora, caught off guard, looked to Becky for help. For once, the young attorney was speechless.

Cora turned back to Harper. "That is so nice of you," she improvised. "Bringing us a copy. I assure you we won't tell Ratface you did."

"No, no," Harper said. "This isn't *your* copy. It's my copy. I brought it to you to solve."

"Oh."

"So, come on. Solve it for me. Let's see what it says."

Cora bit her lip. "I can't solve this."

"Why not?"

"Come on, Chief. I'm working for the defense. I'll probably be a witness. What's it going to look like on the stand when Becky brings out how the police coerced me into aiding the prosecution?" Cora shrugged. "Unless you think it will be *detrimental* to the prosecution's case. Don't worry. I won't tell Ratface you told us."

Harper scowled. "Why are you doing this? I thought we were friends."

"We are friends. One friend to another, I'm giving you a little friendly advice. If you want to stay out of trouble, take this puzzle to Harvey Beerbaum. If there's nothing in it that Ratface wouldn't want you to tell us, bring it back and I'll be happy to discuss it. Ratface won't be mad at you for helping the defense, and Becky won't be mad at me for helping the prosecution."

Cora smiled and spread her hands. "Win-win."

Cora was on the computer comparison shopping for underwear. Her panties had begun to feel a little tight. She decided to buy one size larger, just to see how they felt. She found the ones she wanted; now she was looking for free shipping. It was hard to get free shipping on a single pair. But not impossible. With a little work, Cora realized, she could get just about anything.

The phone rang. She scooped it up. "Hello?"

"Cora, it's Becky. Have you heard from Chief Harper?"

"No. Why?"

"He never came back. From Harvey Beerbaum's. Which has to mean something. He'd have come back unless there was something in the puzzle he didn't want us to know."

"He wouldn't do that."

"Why not? You put the idea in his head, saying he could get in trouble for showing us the puzzle."

"I had to give him some reason for refusing to solve it."

"Well, you didn't have to give him that one."

"It's not like I had time to pick and choose: 'Solve this.' 'No.' 'Why not?' 'Ah—I never solve puzzles on Thursday.' "

"It's Wednesday."

"See, I'd have blown it. Becky, it's done, I said it, I'm sorry if you don't like it, but it's kind of where we are."

"Maybe Harvey Beerbaum kept a copy."

"I doubt it."

"Wouldn't he remember what it said? Doesn't he have a mind like a computer?"

"Yeah, but he's not going to tell you."

"Why not?"

"Because Chief Harper brought it to him so the defense wouldn't see it. You think Harvey's going to turn around and show it to us?"

"Damn."

"Don't worry, we'll find out sooner or later."

Cora hung up and drove straight to Chief Harper's office.

The chief was on the phone. He covered the mouthpiece and hissed, "Shh!" He uncovered the phone, said, "No, no, I understand. Believe me, I'm running down every possible lead. I've got a call on the other line." He hung up the phone and said, "You've got a lot of nerve."

"*I've* got a lot of nerve? You took the puzzle and never came back."

"You didn't want to solve it for me."

"So Becky wouldn't have an ethical conundrum and you wouldn't get in trouble for showing us."

"Ethical conundrum?"

"Yeah. Becky suffers from them. Terrible disease. And no one marches for it."

"Cora."

"That was Ratface, wasn't it? That's why you're upset. You don't want him to know I'm in your office."

Harper said nothing, glared at her.

"There was obviously something in the puzzle he wants you to investigate. Which you're already doing. Evidenced by that 'call' on your other line. What *are* you doing about the new lead, Chief?"

"There's no new lead."

"Right. The crossword puzzle was a recipe for fruitcake."

Harper exhaled noisily. He jerked open his desk drawer, took out a paper. "This is the puzzle. I can't let you see it. It would get me into an incredible amount of trouble."

"I can be discreet," Cora said.

"Your discretion is the type that comes with a wrecking ball. I'm sorry, but I just can't do it. I hope you understand." Harper put the puzzle down on his desk. "Anyway, I'm glad you're here. I wanted to talk to you. Do me a favor. Hang on a minute. I gotta give Dan some instructions."

Harper got up and went out. The minute he was gone Cora jumped up and grabbed the crossword puzzle.

She read the theme answer:

You missed
It by a mile
Look at who
Is on trial.

Cora heard footsteps. She quickly replaced the puzzle and sat down in her seat.

Harper came in, closing the door behind him. "I think I set him straight." He sat down at his desk. "Now then, what were we talking about?"

"You had something you wanted to tell me."

"Oh," Harper said. He picked up the puzzle, opened his desk drawer, dropped it in. "What?"

"I don't know, because you didn't tell me."

"I can't remember." Harper shrugged. "It couldn't have been that important. Anyway, I'd like your opinion."

"On what?"

"The case, of course. Never mind if Henry Firth has sufficient evidence or not, what do you think of the case?"

"You're asking this of a member of the defense team," Cora pointed out.

"Right."

"And you're asking it as a member of the prosecution team. That's a sticky situation."

"Yes, it is," Harper said. "So, what do you think? If the defendant didn't do it, who should I be looking at?"

The only real answer was the girlfriend. It was the most logical answer to the question, and it was the answer that most helped Becky's client. It was also the only one Cora could think of at the moment, which put it pretty damn high on the list of possible answers. If only it weren't likely to get her in trouble for blackmail.

Cora was tempted to say "Billy the Bug." But she'd caused the poor man enough trouble, finessing Rick Reed into asking about him on television. And the chief had already shot the idea down in no uncertain terms.

Cora hesitated.

"Come on," Harper said. "You say Brittany Wells didn't do it, who do you think should be on trial?"

Cora took a breath.

"I have no idea."

Sergeant Crowley wasn't answering his phone. Nothing new there. Cora wasn't sure if she wanted to drive all the way into the City and run the risk of bumping into Stephanie. Somehow that thought just kind of took the edge off her ardor.

She was hopelessly torn. She started, stopped several times. Got bundled up, went out to the car, thought better of it, went back inside, shrugged off her overcoat, and made herself a cup of coffee. "Made" was perhaps too strong a word. Cora didn't brew herself one. There was coffee left over from a pot Sherry had made, and Cora zapped it in the microwave. She drank it, wondered belatedly if it was decaffeinated. She didn't really want to be kept up late with bad thoughts bouncing around her head.

Aw, hell.

Cora pulled on her overcoat, got in the car, and headed for New York.

She got as far as the mall. She pulled up in front of Target, went in and bought a Samsung 37-inch high-definition TV set, went home, and set it up in her bedroom.

Buddy was pleased to see her but confused by the television. He loved the box, though, so much so she hated to take it away from him. She left it in the living room for him to play with.

Of course the TV wouldn't work without a converter box, but Cora had bought a fifty-foot roll of cable. She ran it down the hall-way and hooked it up to the cable box on the TV in the living room. She went back in her bedroom and turned on her new TV.

It was beautiful! In your face, Sherry Carter. You think you're the only one with a TV in the bedroom, well, think again.

The only problem was Cora couldn't change the channel without going back in the living room and zapping the converter box with the remote. She'd call the cable company in the morning, get them to come out. If they tried to stall her off, maybe she'd tell them she was the Puzzle Lady. Cora didn't abuse her celebrity status often, but for something as important as a TV remote you didn't have to jump out of bed and run into the other room to use it was surely excusable.

Particularly when that TV was small consolation for a New York cop with a girlfriend.

Cora went in the living room, disconnected the cable, reconnected the living room TV, picked up the remote, and flipped through the channels. She found a Knicks game. They were playing the Miami Heat. Excellent.

She disconnected the TV, reconnected the cable, went back in the bedroom where the Knicks now graced her new television, and flopped down on the bed to watch. Buddy hopped up beside her. Ah. This was the life.

She lay there, watching the Knicks, and fantasizing that she actually *had* a remote control, that she could change channels during the commercials. Or at least mute them. Boy, there would be a lot of things she could do then.

The phone rang.

Cora scowled. The Knicks had just put on a twelve-point run to take a seven-point lead, not the time for an interruption. It occurred to Cora if she had a zapper and a DVR she could freeze the game right there and pick it up when the annoying phone call was over.

Cora reached for the nightstand, grabbed the phone. "Hello?"

"Cora, it's Becky."

"Not a good time, Becky."

"What, is he there?"

"Who?"

"Crowley."

"No," Cora said a little more sharply than she intended.

"Sorry to bother you. I got work."

"Good for you."

"No, I got work for *you*."

"So call me in the morning."

"It can't wait."

"What?"

"Brittany Wells called. She wants you back."

"*What?*"

"She's scared. She wants protection."

"You're kidding."

"She thinks she's in danger. She's afraid whoever killed her husband will try to kill her."

"Why in the world would she think that?"

"Who knows why that woman thinks anything? Somehow she got it in her head that if her husband didn't profit from the insurance policy, he didn't accidently kill himself trying to kill her. So someone else must have killed him. So maybe she's next."

"She's out of her mind."

"That may well be. But that's more logic than I would have given her credit for. Anyway, she wants you on the job. Starting now. Seeing as how she's my only paying client at the moment, I'd rather not tell her to go to hell. So, whaddya say?"

Cora ground her teeth. She really didn't want to do it. But she felt guilty about not telling Becky about the puzzle Chief Harper had "accidently" let her get a look at. It had been a tough call, just whose friendship she was going to abuse, whose loyalty she was going to violate.

Harper had put her in a hell of a position. To tell or not to tell.

Not to tell had won out, largely because telling was irreparable. There was no way to *un*tell. Whereas the decision not to tell could be reversed at any time. If the case ever went to trial and Brittany was in danger of being convicted, it would be another matter. The way things stood, there was no upside in delivering the message.

Except for the danger factor. Brittany was afraid her husband's death hadn't been an accident, that there was a killer. Her belief was based on her fear that there was a killer and he wasn't her. The puzzle said that there was a killer and it wasn't her. Since Cora was suppressing the fact that there was a basis for her apprehension, could she really ignore her cries for help?

On her new TV, the Heat had rallied, tied it up.

Cora sighed.

"Aw, hell."

Cora felt weird driving up to Brittany's house. It occurred to her she could park in the driveway because she didn't have to leave room for Hank's car. The thought freaked her out enough she didn't want to do it. She parked in the street as she had before and walked up the drive. As she did she had the creepy feeling she was being watched. She felt stupid. There was no one around, and no one was watching her, unless Brittany was peeking out the window. Even so, Cora slipped her hand into her drawstring purse and gripped her gun. Which make her feel more foolish.

Brittany met her at the door as if it were just another social occasion. "Hi, thanks for coming, why don't you sit down in the living room, I'm just making coffee," she said, and vanished into the kitchen.

Cora counted to ten, at the end of which she had talked herself out of turning around and walking out the door. Instead, she went in the living room and installed herself on the couch, and a few minutes later she and Brittany were having coffee together just as they had the time before.

It was strange being Brittany's bodyguard again. It had been strange protecting her from her husband. Now that he was dead, it wasn't just strange; it was eerie. Who was she protecting her from? Some unknown assassin of Brittany's own making. A figment of her imagination.

Cora sat on the couch sipping coffee and wondering how one shot a figment.

"Silver bullets," Cora murmured.

Brittany frowned. "What?"

"Sorry. My mind was wandering. It does that now and then."

"I know you think this is silly."

"Hey, kid, it's your money."

"Not yet," Brittany said.

Cora raised her eyebrows. Had Brittany made a joke? No, the woman was dead serious. It wasn't her money yet. Maybe she deserved a little more consideration as a suspect.

"Who are you afraid of?" Cora said.

"I don't know. I don't know who's doing this. If I did, it wouldn't be so scary."

"Or it might be scarier," Cora said.

"Huh?" Brittany said.

"You're imagining someone scary. That's your expectation. When you find out who it is, he may be worse than you imagined. That would be scarier."

Brittany thought that over. Cora could practically see her mind working. If so, it was working very slowly. Eventually, it processed Cora's remark and came to a conclusion. "You're weird."

"Yeah, but I make up for it by being a very good shot," Cora said. "Now then, tell me, who are *you* having an affair with?"

Brittany's mouth fell open. "I beg your pardon!"

"Well, your husband's gone all day. You think he's cheating on you. Naturally you'd want a little payback. So who's the lucky guy?"

"I was *not* cheating on my husband," Brittany said indignantly.

"Really? You were a good girl. Well, that certainly was a waste now, wasn't it? Now that he's dead."

"Why are you being so rude?"

"Sorry," Cora said. "Just trying to determine how much you want my services. If you weren't really afraid of something, you'd have thrown me out of here by now."

"This is not a game."

"I know. Even so, there's winners and losers. If you want to be a winner, you might try leveling with your lawyer."

"You're not my lawyer."

"You want me to call her, get her over here? You can tell both of us."

"There's nothing to tell."

Cora studied her face. "Yes, there is. Something about the death of your husband terrifies you. I don't know what it is, so clearly you haven't told us everything."

"I don't need a lecture."

"You need something."

"Not from you. What do you know? You ever have your husband killed on you?"

"Almost," Cora said.

"Your husband was almost killed?"

"No, he *was* killed. He was *almost* my husband. He was killed before we got to the altar."

"Oh."

Brittany lapsed into silence.

"So, where am I going to sleep?" Cora said.

Brittany looked as if she hadn't considered it. "Sleep?"

"You expect me to sit outside your bedroom door with a gun in my lap all night?"

"Of course not. There's another room across the hall. I think there's sheets on the bed."

"You *think*?"

"I'm pretty sure. If there aren't, we must have some."

"Great." Cora got up from the couch.

"You're going to bed *now*?" Brittany said.

"Well, I'm not going to sit up yacking all night."

"It's early. Wanna watch some TV?"

"I don't suppose you're a Knicks fan," Cora said.

"Huh?"

"Game's probably over anyway."

Brittany's TV wasn't as good as the one Cora just bought, but it had the advantage of having the remote in the same room. Cora picked it up, turned on the TV and flipped through the channels. *Law & Order* was on—no surprise there, *Law & Order* was *always* on. Cora wondered if she could stand watching New York City cops, figured she'd better get used to it.

"This okay?" Cora said.

Brittany didn't seem interested. "Whatever," she said.

At eleven Cora switched over to *The Daily Show*. Jon Stewart was doing a particularly funny segment. Cora enjoyed it immensely, but she wished they didn't have to bleep him. Brittany seemed preoccupied, didn't react at all. Or to Stephen Colbert, or to David Letterman when Cora joined the show in progress at twelve. Brittany was wound up, distracted, and tense, was constantly jumping up, checking the door, checking the windows, pacing in and out of the room. It was enough to drive a normal person nuts. Cora was beginning to despair of ever going to bed.

Midway through the Craig Ferguson show Brittany's eyelids began to seem a little heavy and her chin slumped forward on her chest.

The phone rang and she jumped a mile.

"Oh, my God! What's that?"

"It's the phone," Cora said dryly. The explanation seemed somewhat unnecessary—the phone was still ringing. "Well, aren't you going to answer it?"

Brittany backed away from the phone as if it were alive. "It's him! I know it's him!"

"Don't be silly."

"Who else would call this time of night?"

"I don't know. You can find out by picking up the phone."

Brittany steeled herself, reached out, grabbed the phone. "Hello?" she said tentatively. The expression on her face changed. She lowered the receiver from her ear, looked at Cora. "It's for you."

"This is stupid," Sam Brogan said.

For once Cora agreed with Bakerhaven's crankiest police officer. He'd been sent to babysit Brittany Wells so Cora could leave her post.

"Let her make you some coffee, Sam. She likes to make coffee."

Cora got in the car and drove out to 415 Fairview. She didn't recognize the address, but she recognized the house. She'd been driving past it for years without knowing who lived there. It was painted pale yellow, which was why she remembered it. Most houses in Bakerhaven were white.

Dan Finley met her at the front door. He lowered his voice. "He's in a very bad mood."

"Figures," Cora said.

"Dan!" Chief Harper yelled from inside.

Dan gave Cora an I-told-you-so look and ducked back through the door. Cora followed him in.

The house was small by any standards, the equivalent of a New York City studio apartment, and the living room was a bandbox.

In the middle of the ceiling an old metal fan in a circular wire protective frame was twisted askew and nearly pulled out of its mounting.

A rope hung from the fan. It was a piece of clothesline. It hung straight, but the end looked as if it had been twisted.

Billy the Bug lay on his back under the rope. His face was purple, his tongue protruded from his mouth, and his eyes bulged out of his head.

Chief Harper knelt over the body. As Dan came in he stood up and said, "Good. Take your pictures so these guys can get him out of here."

An EMS unit standing by with a gurney was talking to Dr. Nathan. Despite the hour, Barney wore a red bow tie, his standard crime scene attire. He had made a preliminary examination of the body and was just waiting for the EMS boys to cart it off to the morgue for him to autopsy.

Harper turned to Cora, said accusingly, "Well?"

"Well, what?"

"How did you know it was him?"

"I didn't know it was him. He seemed a likely suspect, but you talked me out of it."

Harper scowled. "I *didn't* talk you out of it. It was a stupid idea then, and it's a stupid idea now. I don't know how it happened to be true, but it defies the laws of logic. It's one of those things that just aren't fair."

"I'm sure Billy would agree."

"Don't try to be funny."

"I wasn't trying to be funny."

Harper held up a plastic evidence bag. "This was on the floor. You know what it is?"

"A TV zapper?"

"Not for our cable system."

"Remote-control detonator?"

"More likely."

"All set, Chief," Dan said.

"You done with the pictures?"

"I'm done with the body. I still got the crime scene."

"I know that. I meant the body. Okay, Barney, he's all yours. Call me when you're done."

"Sure," Barney said. "But I can tell you right now, you got no problem with the time." He followed the gurney out.

"What did he mean by that?" Cora said.

Harper sighed. "Take a look."

On one side of where the body had lain was a small desk with a computer. There was a straight-backed chair in front of it. The chair was facing away from the desk, not that far from the hanging rope.

Cora leaned around the chair, looked at the computer.

An e-mail program was on the screen. It was open to the sent-mail file. The last letter sent was on the screen. It was addressed to the Bakerhaven Police Department.

The letter read:

I never meant to kill anyone. I just wanted to see the fire.
I can't live with this.
I'm pressing Send and stepping off the chair.

Brittany was animated. More than animated, she was reborn. The timid, morose, paranoid idiot had been replaced by an exuberant, confident, decisive idiot, a type Cora knew well and immediately categorized as megabitch.

Brittany strode around Becky's office as if it were a battleground and she were Henry V, heartening the troops. "See?" Brittany said. "Everyone thought I was crazy, but someone *was* after me. I was right and you were wrong. I was right all the time."

"He wasn't after you," Cora said irritably.

"And *you've* got to get my money back," she said, pointing a finger at Becky. "You've gotta go down to the courthouse and tell them I didn't do it and I want my money back."

"It's not that easy," Becky said.

"I didn't do it! Now they know I didn't do it, and they've got no right to say I did. They took all my money for that bail thing, and I've got nothing to live on, and that's not right. So get it now, because there's some things I need to buy."

"I will petition the court in your behalf," Becky said.

"'Petition the court'? What the hell does that mean? Another hearing. I don't want another hearing. I just want my money."

"Of course you do," Cora said. "And she's going to get it for you. But she has to do it by legal means. Otherwise it's known as stealing."

"You think it's funny? It's not funny. How'd you feel if someone took all your money for something you didn't do?"

It occurred to Cora that as the Puzzle Lady she was *paid* for something she didn't do. "That would be rather ironic."

Cora realized belatedly that Becky didn't know her deception extended to the creative side of puzzles, but she doubted that even her astute legal mind would get the enigmatic in-joke.

Brittany rode right though Cora's comment. "We get the money back, and we get them to say they made a mistake and I didn't do it and they're not going to put me on trial. Then we make the insurance company pay up. You tell them I didn't do it and they have to give me the money."

"I will petition the insurance company on your behalf."

"'Petition'? What is this petition? It's my money. I want it. Tell them they have to pay it."

"I will tell them," Becky said. "But they will tell me they have to investigate the claim."

"'Investigate'? What do you mean, 'investigate'?"

"Any claim of that size they're going to investigate thoroughly before paying up."

"Who is?"

"The insurance company."

"You keep saying that. That's not an answer. The insurance company isn't a person. It's a company. *Who* is going to investigate?"

"Insurance companies employ private investigators to check out large claims to see if there's anything fraudulent about them."

"Fraudulent?"

"For God's sake, Becky," Cora said irritably. "Put it in words of one syllable. Look, kid, they won't pay up till they make sure you're not faking. You know, like is a guy's leg really broken or is he just pretending it is? They send out a private detective to snap some pictures of him playing tennis on that broken leg. See what I mean?'

Brittany looked baffled. "Tennis?"

"Bad example. Look. Your insurance policy is double indemnity. You understand that, right? The policy pays a million dollars if your husband dies, two million if his death is an accident."

"And it was! So they owe two million."

"Right. But they're not going to take your word for it. They want to make sure it was an accident."

"But it was. This guy didn't mean to kill him; he just did."

"Right," Cora said. "Sort of. It would still be an accident even if he meant to kill him."

"How can it be an accident if he did it on purpose?"

"As far as *your husband's* concerned, it's an accident. *He* didn't know he was going to be murdered."

"They still have to pay if he was murdered?"

"Unless you killed him."

"Otherwise they have to pay?"

"Absolutely. They can't get out of it by proving Billy really meant to kill him."

"So if she can get the police to say I didn't do it, then they have to pay."

"There's one other instance where they wouldn't have to pay," Becky said.

Brittany looked at her suspiciously. "Hey, whose side are you on?"

"She's on your side," Cora snapped. "You want her to tell you the truth, or you want her to tell you what you want to hear?"

"Hey!" Brittany stared her down. "I was *talking* to my *lawyer!*" She turned back to Becky. "Why wouldn't they have to pay?"

"If your husband blew himself up so you could collect the insurance money, he killed himself for nothing."

"You mean if he was trying to rig the bomb to kill me and it went off and killed him, they wouldn't have to pay?"

"No, it's still an accidental death. They don't have to pay if it's a *suicide*. If he *meant* to kill himself."

"But he didn't. The firebug blew him up with a remote device. And he killed himself, and now everyone knows I didn't do it!" Brittany's eyes gleamed as she warmed to the premise. "And I get everything! The house and the car—too bad there's only one—and whatever money's kicking around, and, oh, I get the bail money back! And then I'll get the two million from the insurance company! What else? I was arrested and I didn't do it—can't I sue somebody for that?"

Cora didn't wait to hear the answer. She turned and slammed out the door.

Cora flounced into Cushman's Bake Shop. Screw the diet. Screw the weight problem. Screw the fact that she'd already had breakfast. What difference would another latte and scone make?

Becky's client was infuriating. Cora wanted to scratch her eyes out, even more than she wanted to scratch the eyes out of some of Melvin's girlfriends, and that was a lot. A frightened Brittany Wells was just laughable. A triumphant Brittany Wells was insufferable. It was like listening to some moronic buffoon with an IQ of 67 crowing about how smart he was to have picked the numbers that won the $87 million lottery. Eventually *someone* wins, you idiot. Smart number picking had nothing to do with it.

The shop was crowded, and there were two women ahead of her on line. Cora was torn between elbowing the women out of the way and saying, "Screw it," driving to the Country Kitchen, and ordering a double scotch on the rocks. Was there a 12-step program that covered this situation? There probably was. A support group for private detectives quitting smoking while dealing with murder/suicides.

Mrs. Cushman finished making a latte and rang the woman up. Now she was second in line. She could wait, couldn't she?

"Cora Felton?"

Cora turned.

A plump, matronly woman barreled up to her. Cora instinctively took a step back. The woman was clearly distraught. She looked vaguely familiar, though Cora couldn't place her. Could she be a remnant from her drinking days? An aggrieved wife whose husband she'd made a play for? No, the woman was too old. Though Cora winced at that glass house.

"Yes?" Cora said as tentatively and noncommittally as possible.

The woman's face twisted and tears welled. "Can you help me?"

Relieved that the woman wasn't attacking her and that the customer in front of her had only bought a cranberry muffin and was already done, Cora help up her hand. "Just a minute." She turned to the counter, ordered a latte and a scone.

While Mrs. Cushman made the latte, Cora kept her back to the woman and tried to compose her thoughts. Could she take a case now? Yes, she could. Becky's case was over. Brittany Wells was gone, and good riddance. It would be nice to have something new to tackle, even if this woman couldn't pay, which it looked like she couldn't. It wasn't about the money right now, it was about hanging on to her sanity and not wanting to smoke or to stuff herself with scones until she looked like the Stay Puft man.

Cora paid her bill, picked up her latte and scone, turned back to the potential client. "All right, what do you want?"

"I'm Mrs. Wilson. Billy Wilson's mother."

Cora felt a hollow feeling in the pit of her stomach. And she had made the woman stand and wait.

There were no tables in Cushman's Bake Shop, just counters with cream and sugar and coffee lids. In the summer there were benches out front. In the winter it was too cold. Women sometimes stood and chatted near the counters, but the shop was small. That wouldn't do.

"Come outside," Cora said.

That confused Mrs. Wilson. "Huh?"

"Come on."

Cora's car was parked in front of the library. She installed Mrs. Wilson in the front seat, started the car, and turned on the heater. She sipped her coffee, trying to think how to begin.

"I'm sorry for your loss."

Tears welled in the woman's eyes. "I don't understand."

Cora opened her mouth, closed it again. Realized the woman wasn't responding to her remark. Once again Cora couldn't think of what to say. She decided any prompt would do. "Tell me."

"Billy wouldn't do that. He wouldn't. It doesn't make any sense. He had a problem. A big problem. Everyone knew. But he beat it. Put it behind him. Been working ever since to live it down. Why in the world would he do something like that? It's not like him. It makes no sense. He didn't know anything about explosives. He set fire with sticks and gasoline. He poured gasoline on wood. He didn't blow up cars."

Cora suddenly realized they were sitting in a car in almost the same spot where Hank Wells blew up. An awfully tactless thing to have done to this poor woman. Was she commenting on it? No, the woman was oblivious, lost in her own train of thought.

"Billy wasn't living with you, right? Hadn't been for years?"

"Yes."

"There might be things you don't know about him. People can change."

Mrs. Wilson snuffled. Stuck out her jaw. Looked at Cora. "You have children?"

"No."

"Then you don't know. I'm a mother. I know my boy. He couldn't lie to me. He still can't." She corrected herself. "Still *couldn't*. It's not like I didn't see him. I saw him all the time. He came to dinner once a week. I always asked him, 'How are you doing? Is anything bothering you? Is anything wrong?' And there wasn't. He could not have blown up that car."

"Could he have killed himself?" Cora said gently.

"I don't know. I don't know. He was very upset about that TV reporter. What he said to the police. Very upset. He went into his shell."

"But the police said he didn't do it."

"Of course they did. Because he didn't. Of course he didn't do it. You know it; I know it; the police know it; everybody in the world knows it. The TV reporter probably knows it, but he wanted to get a good sound bite." Mrs. Wilson spit the words out. "He was despondent. Can you blame him?"

"Do you think he hung himself?"

"No. He might have done it; he felt bad enough to. But he wouldn't have typed that note. About the car bomb. About killing that man. Because he didn't do it. So he couldn't have hung himself. Because he wouldn't have said he did. Unless he snapped completely. Unless hearing that TV reporter say he did confused him, made him think he was losing his mind, that he'd actually done it and just couldn't remember. And he *was* losing his mind, only not that he didn't remember, but that he *thought* he didn't remember. That's the only way it would make sense."

Cora's latte and scone were long forgotten. She heaved a huge sigh. "What do you want me to do?"

"Nothing can bring my boy back. But having people think ill of him is too much. Whether he hung himself or not, he didn't set that car bomb. And the police aren't going to do anything about it. They have his confession; what more do they want? But it's not true. I'm telling you it's not true. You've found things out before. I know you have. Things the police didn't. Someone needs to stick up for my boy. Show he didn't do this terrible thing. Can you do that? Not for me. For him. Because it isn't fair. And life should be fair, shouldn't it? I know it isn't, but it should be. This is a horrible injustice that needs to be fixed. So can you do it? Please."

Tears welled in Cora's eyes. She felt like her head was going to come off. She wanted to tell the woman, yes, of course she'd help her. But she couldn't lie to her. It was bad enough withholding the fact that she was responsible for Rick Reed's question. She couldn't compound the crime by promising something she didn't think she could deliver.

Cora couldn't meet the woman's eyes. "I don't know."

Chapter

5 0

Becky came down the stairs from her office just as Cora emerged from the alley behind the pizza parlor. She looked guilty.

"What were you doing?" Becky said.

"I was just coming to see you."

"You just left."

"I was coming back."

"In the alley?"

"I wasn't in the alley."

"Yes, you were."

"I was in the pizza parlor. I know I shouldn't eat pizza, but I can't help myself."

"Uh-huh," Becky said. She pushed by Cora, looked down the alley.

Wisps of smoke hung in the air.

Becky wheeled on Cora. "You were smoking!"

"No, I wasn't."

Becky thrust out her hand. "Gimme."

"Give you what?"

"Give me your cigarettes."

"I don't have any cigarettes."

"You worked so hard. You were doing so well. You can't blow it now."

Cora scowled at Becky defiantly. She groped in her drawstring purse as if she were going to pull out her gun and shoot Becky in the face. Instead she yanked out a pack of cigarettes and slapped them into Becky's hand. "Satisfied?"

"No, I'm not," Becky said. "Come back upstairs and tell me what's the matter."

Cora glowered at her.

"What you gonna do, buy another pack of cigarettes? Either go see a therapist or talk to me. You can't just hide and smoke."

"Aw, hell."

Cora turned and marched up the stairs like an unruly pupil on her way to the principal's office.

Becky followed her in, sat her down, closed the door. "Now then, why are you smoking?"

"Are you kidding me? It's a wonder I'm not drinking."

"So Crowley's got a girlfriend. It's not like you've never dealt with *that* before. How long have you been smoking? Ever since you found out?"

"That's not it."

"So. What's wrong?"

"I killed a man."

Becky's face softened. "Cora. That was a long time ago. He was an evil man. He deserved to die."

Cora shook her head. "No, no, no. Not *him*. Don't you understand? I killed Billy the Bug."

"Oh, for goodness' sakes."

"I did. I got Rick Reed to ask Chief Harper about it on the air. That's what drove the poor man over the edge. Hearing a TV reporter ask the cops if he was a suspect. I did that. Brought up his past sins and threw them in his face. Hounded an innocent man into killing himself."

"Yes, but he wasn't innocent," Becky said.

"Which doesn't make any sense. Why would Billy burn a car in broad daylight? He hasn't burned anything in years."

"He hasn't been *caught* in years."

"And he never used a car bomb before."

"Changing his MO would be a reason he hadn't been caught."

"Stop it. You're being me again. Countering emotional reactions with logic."

"Someone has to," Becky said. "You're blowing this out of proportion."

"Out of proportion? Becky, the man's dead. And then I have to listen to that looney tunes troop around your office like a demented diva."

"I can't even sort out that image. Calm down. Take a breath. Realize the whole world does not revolve around you."

"That isn't remotely what I was saying."

"You're taking credit for a sick man's suicide."

"If it *was* suicide."

"What are you talking about?'

"What if he was framed?"

"'Framed'? How do you frame a firebug?" Becky shook her head. "That sounds like one of those mysteries you read. *The Framed Firebug.*"

"It's not funny, Becky. I may not be functioning at full capacity, but I look at this case, and everything about it reeks to high heaven. A guy who used to burn buildings inexplicably firebombs a car. Coincidentally, killing the husband of a woman who just found out he has a two-million-dollar life insurance policy on his head."

"You think my client planned this?"

"I don't think your client could plan a dinner party. But she's the one who profits most from his death."

"You think she killed her husband?"

"Or tricked Billy the Bug into doing it."

"Which you don't think she's smart enough to do."

"No."

"So how does it work?"

Cora glared at Becky. "I can't do this without a cigarette."

"Then you can't do it at all. Consider yourself fired."

"Becky."

"You want to talk this out, fine. You're not smoking in my office."

"Fine. All right, here's the deal. If Billy the Bug was set up—boy, I never thought I'd hear that line outside of a forties noir movie—it happens one of two ways. Either he has nothing to do with the bombing and was framed, or he was duped into setting the bomb with no idea anyone was going to be killed."

"Which conspiracy theory do you like?"

"You're making fun of me."

"You're ridiculing anything that helps my client. You expect me to sit and applaud?"

"No, but I'd like you to listen. Or let me go back to the alley."

"Go on."

"Doesn't it strike you as too pat? The murderer confesses and kills himself, conveniently leaving the murder weapon in plain sight. The suicide note is not handwritten, but sent e-mail. E-mail, for God's sake."

"So the police would find him and cut him down. Or he might have hung there until he began to rot."

"What does he care? He's dead. He killed himself in a fit of remorse after blowing someone up when all he meant to blow up was a car."

"When you put it like that, it sounds stupid," Becky admitted.

"Well then, you put it so it doesn't. The problem is I can't figure a scenario that works. The Bug's in cahoots with your client and blows up her husband as part of some prearranged plan, then has a change of heart. The Bug kills her husband by mistake, the odds of which happening are only slightly worse than those of winning the New York Lottery. The Bug's in cahoots with the husband, kills him accidentally, and kills himself. The Bug's in cahoots with the husband, who kills *himself* accidentally, and kills himself anyway." Cora waved her hands alongside of her head. "It's hard to imagine which of those are worse."

"No kidding."

Cora spread her arms. "So there you are. Logically, Billy the Bug was framed. In which case he was also killed."

"I like that theory," Becky said.

"Why?"

"Because my client didn't do it. She was with you when it happened."

"I suppose."

"What do you mean, you suppose? Did you ever let her out of your sight? Long enough to drive into town and kill someone? By standing him on a chair and putting a rope around his neck? And writing an e-mail on his computer?"

"No, but—"

"There's no buts about it. She couldn't have done it."

"She could have stood him on a block of ice that melted and hung him while she was with me, giving her a perfect alibi."

"Are you kidding me?"

"Yes. There was no water on the floor. She also would have had to arrange it so that in falling he hit the Send icon on the computer, e-mailing his confession to the cops."

"So my client is cleared."

"Of killing Billy the Bug, I should say so. Her husband is another matter."

"If she killed her husband, who killed the firebug?"

"I did."

"Cora."

"Well, that's what makes the most sense. She tricked the firebug into killing her husband, and I pushed the poor man into taking his own life."

"You're determined to take the blame."

"I'm not. I don't think that happened, either. It's just the most likely of a bunch of unlikely possibilities."

"What's a *likely* possibility?"

"There *are* none. The only thing that makes sense is that the husband planned the crime."

"What?"

"Only it doesn't make sense because, A, the insurance policy wasn't on his wife, and, B, he's dead."

"What if he blew himself up trying to kill her?"

"Then the insurance policy would be on his wife. The only way it works is if the body in the car wasn't him."

"But it is."

"I know. I had hope when it was just a charred body in a car. But dental records don't lie. Hank Wells is no more. Brittany Wells is a widow. Unless she happened to kill Hank, what's his is hers. Not to mention the two-million-dollar pot of gold at the end of the rainbow."

"Brittany didn't kill anyone."

"I can see why you'd like to hold on to that theory."

"Cora. You were with her all night when Billy was killed. And you were standing next to her in the police station when her husband blew up. You still think she did it?"

"No. But I don't think Billy did, either. Someone else did. It's up to us to find out who."

"No, it isn't."

"The police aren't going to investigate. They think the case is closed."

"Cora. If the case is closed, my client gets two million dollars. Do you know what a third of two million dollars is? My fee."

"If Billy didn't do it, it will be a huge miscarriage of justice."

"I got news for you. They happen all the time. I can't automatically reject one because it happens to be in my favor."

"Fine."

Becky studied Cora's face. "You don't think it's fine, do you? You're gonna go off and work the case yourself. You can't do that. You're working for my client. Your work may be done, but that doesn't mean you can rush out and do something that would undermine her best interests. Do you understand? It would be unethical.

It's a type of thing that would keep you out of the PIs' Hall of Fame."

"It's not funny, Becky."

"No, it's serious. There's two million bucks at stake here. You mess it up, you think my client's not gonna come after you?"

"You'd sue me?"

"I wouldn't sue you, but my client might. She's drunk with power and wants to take on the world. If she wants to sue you, *I can't stop her*. I can drop her as a client, throw a six-figure contingency fee out the window, if that's what you think I ought to do."

"Of course not."

"I'd have to sue her for the work I'd done. And her new lawyer would be sure to point out how much cheaper it would be for her to have them fight against paying me the fee than to actually pay it. See the problem?"

"Yeah."

"My client is a runaway train, and there's no reason for me to throw myself on the track. Unless you make one."

Cora heaved a sigh. "Oh, hell."

Chief Harper scooped up the phone. "Yes, Dan."

"Becky Baldwin's here to see you."

"That can't be good."

It wasn't.

Becky burst into the office and stuck a finger in his face. "Why are you harassing my client?" she demanded.

Harper frowned. "I'm not doing anything to your client."

"Exactly," Becky said.

"You've been hanging around Cora too much. It's starting to rub off."

"Don't change the subject."

"What subject? You haven't broached a subject. You barged in here making threats."

"'Threats' is an actionable word."

Harper winced. "See? You're even discussing grammar."

"That wasn't wordplay," Becky said irritably. "I was citing a legal action you don't want to lay yourself open for."

Harper smiled. "On that point, Counselor, we are in complete agreement. Would you care to sit down?"

"This isn't a social call."

"That's good, because I have this murder."

"You have *two* murders. So far you've only made the mistake of charging my client with one."

"Why are you here?"

"You know *exactly* why I'm here."

"Why don't you tell me anyway, so people don't get the idea I'm omniscient?"

"Billy the Bug just confessed to the murder of Hank Wells."

"There was an e-mail to that effect."

"It exonerates my client."

"You could argue that."

"I don't have to argue that. It's not just reasonable doubt. With that confession, no prosecutor in his right mind is going to try anyone else for the crime."

"It would seem hard to get a conviction," Harper said.

"Then why haven't you dismissed the charges?"

"I can't dismiss charges. That's the job of the county prosecutor."

"Why hasn't he dismissed the charges?"

"You'll have to ask him."

"He's not available. I'm asking you."

"Why are you asking me?"

"You're available."

Harper smiled. "Becky, what's the problem? Your client's not in jail; she's not on trial; she's not in imminent danger."

"I want the bail money back."

"I can't rescind bail. I can't even reduce it. Only Judge Hobbs can do that."

"He won't do it. He says he can't reduce bail on the strength of what Rick Reed says on TV."

"Hard to argue with that," Harper said.

"He says it would take a request from the prosecutor."

"So get a request from the prosecutor."

"He's not available."

Harper smiled. "The wheels of justice grind slowly."

"I demanded a hearing. Judge Hobbs looked at his calendar, scheduled me for a week from Thursday."

"So he didn't deny your request."

"No, it's the pocket veto. The bottom line is, I don't get the money."

"Becky, we're a small town of limited resources. It's standard practice to hang on to any public money as long as possible so it accrues some interest."

"Wonderful. Your position is, 'Yes, you're being robbed; unfortunately, that's public policy.'"

"That's *not* what I said, and you better not quote me on it."

"I'm not quoting you, Chief, but I don't appreciate your attitude, either. You can't have two suspects charged with the same crime."

"Billy isn't charged with the crime."

"He's dead."

"Which is probably why. I admit it's an unfortunate situation. I'm sure it will all be cleaned up eventually."

"Yeah. In the meantime, how's my client supposed to live? On the money the insurance company won't pay out as long as she's charged with the crime?"

"What do you expect me to do about it?"

"Couldn't you put in a call to unavailable Henry Firth, remind him how in this small town we all have to work together in the spirit of cooperation?"

Harper smiled. "Well, you finally asked me something I can answer."

"Thank goodness for that."

"The answer is no."

Chapter

5 2

Cora was sublimating her desire for a cigarette by watching Jennifer cavort around the living room with Buddy. It wasn't working. The antics were amusing, but the high-pitched barks and squeals were setting her teeth on edge. The insistent ringing of the kitchen phone completed the excruciating dissonance.

Cora stomped into the kitchen, nearly jerked the phone off the wall. "Hello!"

It was Becky Baldwin. "Get in here. You're back on the clock."

Cora left Jennifer with Sherry and drove into town. She stopped by Cushman's Bake Shop and bought two lattes and two California buns. She marched into Becky's office, set the coffee on the desk, and pulled the pastries out of the bag.

"What's that?" Becky said.

"Comfort food. You sounded stressed."

"You trying to get me fat?"

"That would comfort *me*," Cora said. "I'm putting on weight. I could use the company."

"No thanks."

"Then I'll have to eat 'em both," Cora said. "You'll feel guilty for making me." She took a bite of the California bun. "Oh, God, it's worth it."

"I'll eat part of one," Becky said. "You happy?"

"You've made my day."

Becky broke off a corner, took a bite. "Oh, that's good! What is it?"

"California bun. Not to be confused with California roll. That's fish. A California bun is basically a croissant dipped in sugar, rolled into a bun, and baked to a honey glaze."

"That ought to be illegal." Becky broke off another bite.

"So what did you want?"

Becky took a sip of latte. "We have to solve the crime."

"Really? What brought you around to that opinion?"

"I got less enthusiastic for the Billy-did-it theory when I found out the court system would use it as a reason for *not* returning the bail money. It turns out I have to find a *live* suspect they can charge with the crime. Billy's dead, so they don't have to charge him."

"That makes sense."

"Whose side are you on?"

"If you're paying me, I'm on yours."

"I'm paying you."

"What are you paying me to do?"

Becky took another bite of California bun. "I'll pay you not to bring me any more of these. I can't stop eating it." She washed it down with latte. "Let's go back to the original premise. Brittany hired me because she was afraid her husband was trying to kill her. We abandoned that premise because he turned out to be the victim."

"Which is a pretty good reason," Cora said. "Not to mention the fact the policy was on him."

"Yeah. Right. But suppose in spite of all that, the premise was true?"

"He's trying to kill his wife even though he doesn't gain anything?"

"But he does."

"Oh, yeah? What does he get?"

"A dead wife."

"How does that help him?"

"It's gets him out of the marriage."

"There are easier ways to dissolve a marriage."

"That's funny, coming from you. When I think about what you've said about some of your divorces. And then there's Melvin."

"What about Melvin?"

"He's still paying you alimony. Hank's young. Maybe he didn't want to spend the rest of his life paying alimony."

"Okay," Cora said. "Then why does he want to get rid of his wife?"

Becky shrugged. "Suppose there *was* another woman?"

Crowley's smile was cautiously guarded. "Hi," he said.

Cora raised her hand and sat down. "Relax. I'm not here to make trouble. I'm in your office, during working hours, neutral territory, neutral time."

"Really?" I thought your case was closed."

"Where did you hear that?"

"Harper said some guy confessed."

"You spoke to Chief Harper?"

"I'm a cop."

"You're a New York City cop. You called him about a Baker-haven case?"

"Actually, he called me."

"That makes even less sense. Why would he call you?"

Crowley became interested in some papers on his desk.

"He thought I'd been acting funny and wanted to know if I was up to anything?" Cora said.

"I think he's just concerned about you," Crowley said.

Cora's eyes widened. "He called to ask about my personal life?"

"He wanted to know if we were having problems."

"You said, no, aside from the fact I'd been replaced by another woman, everything was fine."

"That's not the way it is."

"Oh? How is it?"

"It's complicated."

"It always is. But that's not why I'm here. Like I said, it's not personal; it's business."

"You can never go wrong quoting *The Godfather,*" Crowley said.

"I want to know why the purported New York girlfriend of a Bakerhaven resident who got blown up in a car has a crossword puzzle yielding the address of the guy who blew up."

"Oh, is that all," Crowley said.

"You met this woman face-to-face. What was your impression? Did you think she was telling the truth?"

"I did."

"Okay," Cora said. "So if she had nothing to do with anything, why is she brought into the equation? What is her function? Why is she there?"

"I have no idea."

"Neither have I. And that's significant."

Crowley groaned. "That sounds entirely too much like Sherlock Holmes."

"That doesn't make it wrong. The woman's a dead end. So maybe that's her function. To lead us to a dead end. She's a wrong turn to keep us from taking a right turn."

"Such as?"

"Maybe he had a girlfriend, but it wasn't her. Wouldn't that fill the bill?"

"No, it wouldn't. I've seen the movie *Double Indemnity*; I know how it works. If he had an insurance policy on his wife and he and his girlfriend conspired to kill her, it would work just fine. It would be like the movie with the genders reversed. What we have is *exactly* like the movie. The wife and the agent plot to kill the heavily insured husband."

"That didn't happen here."

"Why not?"

"Because the wife is Becky's client. I'm not trying to convict Becky's client."

"That's the problem. I'm a cop. I have no personal agenda. I'm out to get the bad guy, whoever it may be."

"Fine. You want to hunt for Brittany Wells' insurance agent lover be my guest. Personally, I think it's a waste of time. On the other hand, if you would like to do something more constructive along the lines of some of the points I was raising, I can even suggest a place to start."

"Oh? What's that?"

"Interview the coworkers."

"Why?"

"Because no one did."

Cora stuck her head into the conference room. "That's the last one."

Sergeant Crowley looked up from the long table. "Anybody recognize you?"

Cora had taken her glasses off and tucked her hair into a hat. "If so, they didn't let on. You get anything useful?"

"Not in the least."

"You took notes?"

"I took notes. You can read 'em. You can frame 'em. You can laminate 'em."

"Let's talk to the next to the last guy again."

"Which guy was that?"

"Don't you keep 'em in order?"

"In order to what?"

Cora rolled her eyes.

"What did he look like?" Crowley said.

"The thirtysomething guy with the thin face and the bad haircut."

"There's only one?"

"Crowley."

"Yeah, I know who you mean."

"Have him in again."

"Why?"

"On his way out he looked relieved. And this time, let me sit in."

"On what pretext?"

"I don't need a pretext. These guys think I'm a plainclothes cop."

"Okay."

"You want me to go get him?"

Crowley picked up the phone. "I'll call the switchboard."

"Gonna ask for the guy with the bad haircut?"

Crowley referred to his notes. "I think his name's Rodney Klein."

"What if it isn't?"

"Then I'll ask for someone else."

Rodney Klein was the guy with the bad haircut, but he didn't want to sit down. "Why am I back?" he said defensively.

"In case there was anything you forgot to mention."

"Well, there wasn't."

"Or anything you withheld."

Rodney's mouth fell open. "I didn't withhold anything."

"'Withhold' is a scary word. Let's just say something you were glad you didn't have to talk about."

"I—"

"Yes?"

Rodney's eyes flicked to Cora Felton. He looked back at Sergeant Crowley. "Could I talk to you alone?"

Cora didn't want to leave, but it was the wrong time to make a fuss. She gathered up her things, went back in the hall.

Rodney was out five minutes later. He avoided her eyes as he went by.

Cora went back in the conference room where Crowley was gathering up his papers. "Well, did he tell you?"

"Yes, he did."

"Gonna tell me?"

"Doesn't help."

"Oh?"

"He and Hank Wells had lunch in a topless bar."

"You're kidding. He withheld that vital piece of information?" Cora said sarcastically.

"He didn't think it was important, but it bothered him that he left it out."

"Are you sure that's it?" Cora said. "I got quite a different vibe."

"What?

"He was withholding something, and it wasn't embarrassment."

"I didn't get that."

"Did you ask him if Hank had a girlfriend?"

"Yes. I did."

"Did the question bother him?"

"Not at all."

"I can't help thinking there's something there."

"Too bad he threw you out of the room."

"You could have called me back in after the revelation."

"Why?"

" 'Cause I'm the one who asked you to question him."

"I did. On your advice. I questioned all of them on your advice."

"I didn't know your investigative methods would be so sloppy." Crowley took a breath. "Is this about Stephanie?"

"No."

"It seems like it is. I don't know what you're trying to accomplish. You're just using this as an excuse to take shots at me."

"No, I'm not. I'm trying to solve a murder. I've got limited resources and slim leads. I can't throw any of them away."

"You think this guy can solve the crime? He can't even get a decent haircut. You wanna bring him back in here? I question him a third time, he's gonna clam up tighter than a drum. He's leaning in that direction already, wanting to know what the hell difference it made where he and Hank had lunch. He's just one step away from calling a lawyer and charging police harassment."

"That would be a good indication of guilty knowledge."

"It would be a good indication of why the hell are you picking on me."

"Then bring 'em all back. So the guy won't think it's personal."

"Cora, I have a job. And this isn't it. I'm trying to do you a favor. But I can't guarantee results. Particularly when it's so doubtful there are any to be had. You wanna stick around here and find some excuse to talk to the guy, be my guest. But he's not gonna be receptive. He's seen you with me. It's a case of guilt by association. You're not gonna get to first base."

"I suppose," Cora said. But she didn't look satisfied.

Crowley walked her out. He dawdled on the corner to see if she turned back. From experience he knew it wasn't easy dealing with Cora. There was no telling what she might do. But she stepped out in the street and hailed a cab.

Crowley heaved a sigh of relief and headed for his car.

In Cora's opinion the burning incense was a questionable touch, but otherwise the tapestry shop on Bleecker Street had made a smooth transition into the twenty-first century. Wall hangings shared space with computer terminals on which the shop's Web site featured draperies of all kinds, from theater curtains to company banners to reproductions of works of art. Batik and madras still gave the shop a retro look, in keeping with the West Village address.

Aside from that, the only sixties carryover was the owner herself.

Stephanie's serene demeanor slipped only slightly when Cora walked in. Then she flashed a smile and went back to dealing with her customer, a stylish young woman in the process of renovating a loft. Cora couldn't tell if the woman was an interior decorator or the owner herself. Eventually the sale was completed and duly logged into the computer on the counter and the customer left.

"Well, this is a surprise," Stephanie said.

"Yeah," Cora said. "I didn't tell Crowley I was coming."

"Oh?"

"It's a long story. But if you got time before your next customer . . ."

"It's a walk-in business. I never know."

"Sounds like a precarious way to live. Must be rather nerve-wracking."

"The shop's doing fine. I have online business, too."

"Good for you."

"Yeah. You looking for drapery?"

"Not at the moment."

"I didn't think so. Cora—"

"What?"

"He's not such a bad guy."

"Never said he was."

"I didn't see him the whole time he was with you. I talked to him occasionally, but I didn't see him."

"I'll list it among my accomplishments."

"He's just a little boy."

"Oh, for goodness' sakes!"

"I know. All men are. But in his case, he's a homicide officer. He deals with death all day long."

"Must build up an appetite."

Stephanie glanced at the door. "I'm not sure this is the best place to have this talk."

"You ever close your shop and go to lunch?"

"I have it delivered. I'm a one-woman show."

"But you could if you wanted. You got one of those clocks you hang on the door, says: Back at Two?"

"You wanna go to lunch?"

"No."

"I don't understand."

Cora looked her over, nodded. "You do the earth-mother routine rather well. I know. I used to do it myself. You still do."

"What are you implying?"

"Nothing. Just making a comment. Men like it. Younger men in particular. 'Wow. An uninhibited peace/love hippie. Probably got some good grass.'" Cora's eyes widened. "Oh, my God. That's *your*

Jimi Hendrix poster, isn't it? Crowley just let me think it was his so he wouldn't have to mention you. The whole hippie background, that's your thing. That was never him at all."

Stephanie said nothing, but she didn't look pleased.

"I'm not attacking you, and I'm not criticizing," Cora said. "I'm learning things, and I'm trying to understand. The thing is, you look good. Tall, thin, long hair. You look like the hippie girl guys today wish they'd been around back then to meet."

"What in the world are you talking about?"

"I bet even today you could pull the hippie-chick routine, work your wiles on younger men."

"Is there a point to this?"

"I have a younger man in mind."

"You're fixing me up with someone to get me away from Crowley?"

"No. That would be too low, even for me."

"I don't understand. Who are you trying to fix me up with?"

"A guy with a bad haircut."

Rodney Klein took a sip of scotch and smiled at the older woman sitting next to him at the bar. "What a coincidence," he said.

Stephanie smiled back. "What do you mean?"

"That you should need insurance. I mean, you sit down next to someone at a bar, and what are the odds they have an interest in your business?"

"I have a tapestry shop on Bleecker," Stephanie said. She referred to it as "tapestry" rather than "drapery" or "fabric," to sell the hippie-chick image, the same reason she removed her bra before leaving the shop. She shrugged off her coat to give Rodney the effect of her loose-hanging smock. "I never think of insurance because I have only a few samples in the shop. But there's the client base. I spent years building it up. Now it's all computerized and what if the memory gets wiped?"

"You have backups?"

"Yeah, but an order form got accidently deleted, and guess what wasn't on the memory stick? It was only an order form, no big deal, what if the backup system gets wiped? I have no idea. I need advice."

"We should set up an appointment."

"Would that be with you?"

"It certainly would."

"When would you have time?"

"I'd have to check my appointment book. Ordinarily it would be no problem, but we lost an agent and we're taking up the slack."

"You lost an agent? You mean he quit?"

"Ah, actually it's a little worse than that."

"Oh?"

"He was killed."

"No! How?"

"A car bomb."

"You've gotta be kidding!"

"I'm not."

"It was deliberate?"

"It sure looks like it."

"Why would anyone kill an insurance agent? No offense."

"None taken. I have no idea."

"What do the police think?"

"They don't know, either. They questioned me this afternoon."

"As a witness?"

"No. It happened in Bakerhaven, Connecticut."

"Why did they question you?"

"They're grasping at straws. They don't have a clue."

"What did you tell them?"

"Nothing. Nothing to tell."

"They buy that?"

"It's the truth."

"You didn't know the guy at all?"

"I didn't know anything about him connected to a crime."

"No secret girlfriend? No drugs? Damn. Sex and drugs would be fun."

"Oh."

"Sorry to speak about your friend like that."

"We weren't close. He lived out of town. I saw him at work occasionally." He shook his head. "Poor guy. As if he didn't have enough troubles."

"What do you mean?"

He grimaced. "I shouldn't have said anything. It's not nice to talk behind someone's back."

"Hey. He's dead. He's not going to be offended."

"I guess not. Well, we're salesmen. If we do well, we get commissions. If we don't . . ." He waggled his fingers.

"Your buddy wasn't a very good salesman?"

"No. It was frustrating for him, because he was perfectly personable. He just couldn't close. Some people can't. I've never had a problem. But Hank?" He shook his head again

"Are you sure he didn't have a girlfriend? When it's not going well, a guy wants a shoulder to cry on."

"If he did, he didn't let on."

"And he never asked you to cover for him?"

"What do you mean?"

"You know. Tell his wife he was hung up with a client. Not tell her something."

He frowned. Took another sip of scotch.

"You thought of something?"

"He ducked out of work one afternoon. But it wasn't a woman. He went out to buy something. He said not to mention it."

"Did he tell you what it was?"

"No. Just a present for some kid."

"He had kids. That's sad."

"No, he didn't have kids."

"You sure it was for a kid?"

"Yeah."

"How do you know?"

"Actually, I peeked in the bag."

"What was it?"

"An Iron Man mask."

"I solved your liquor store robbery."

Chief Harper looked up from his desk. "What?"

"I know who did it. You can't arrest him."

"Who did it?"

Cora flopped down in a chair. "Hank Wells. That's why you can't arrest him. He's dead."

"Hank Wells robbed the liquor store?"

"That's right."

"You have proof?"

"No. That's another reason you can't arrest him. But being dead is probably enough."

"Why in the world would an insurance salesman rob a liquor store?"

"I don't know. I just know he did."

"How do you know?"

"Actually, I just suspect."

"How?"

"There's a gray area here, Chief. I'm virtually certain he did it, but I can't tell you how I know. It would get me in trouble."

"You did something illegal."

"Chief. You're asking me to incriminate myself? You haven't even read me my rights."

"I have to warn you, I'm in no mood for this."

"I'm not, either. Nothing about this case is very pleasant. Just between you and me, I don't like our client much. I'm doing the best I can. And I'll help you as much as I can without violating anyone's rights. I'm telling you just as a helpful hint that Hank Wells robbed the liquor store. So you don't waste your time looking for anybody else."

"But you must have some reason for thinking that."

"I do. And I'd feel bad if I didn't tell you about it."

"But you're *not* telling me about it."

"I beg to differ. I didn't bury the lead; I led with the punch line. Hank Wells robbed the liquor store. That's the important fact. How I know is the unimportant fact. It sheds no light on the situation. What you should be asking is why? That's the important question."

"It's one of them. If you ask Ed James—"

"Who?"

"Owner of the liquor store. If you ask him, the important question is where's the money? I don't suppose you have any theories on that?"

"Oh."

"What do you mean, 'oh'?"

"'Theory' is too strong a word. I have an idea."

Harper winced. "Please don't split hairs. You don't have proof Hank Wells robbed the store, but you still think he did. If you think you know where the money is, I'd sure like to know."

"No, you wouldn't. I know Hank robbed the liquor store. I have an idea where the money *may* be. See the difference? You wouldn't like it because it's just a guess. But even if I guess right, you're still not going to like it."

"Oh, yeah. So tell me. Where do you think the money is?"

"I think it blew up."

Cora wasn't so reticent with Becky Baldwin.

"Crowley's girlfriend pumped the witness?" Becky said incredulously.

"Yeah."

"Are you out of your mind?"

"Pretty much. And I have to tell you, it's not a happy high. Withdrawal is no fun, whether it's alcohol, drugs, or merely smoking." She snorted. "'Merely,' hell. Smoking's hardest of all."

"What in the world induced you to use Crowley's girlfriend?"

"I was in a bind. Crowley blew the interview, and was too stubborn to admit it. I couldn't talk to the guy; he thought I was working with Crowley. So I had to run in a ringer. My choices were limited. I don't know a lot of New Yorkers anymore."

"Melvin was busy?"

"Melvin wouldn't have worked."

"I thought Crowley's girlfriend was a lot older than this guy."

"Hey. She's no older than I am."

"That's not what I meant. You made her sound like a call girl."

"Not at all. She's got a peace/love sixties vibe that would appeal to young men's fantasies."

"Earth mother?"

"Exactly. Except on the thin side. Well, not as thin as you."

"So she picked the guy up. What did Crowley have to say about that?"

"Crowley doesn't know."

"You're kidding!"

"It was an awkward situation. He blew the interview. It was like I went over his head."

"You conspired with your ex-boyfriend's current girlfriend to keep secrets from him?"

"What's your point?"

"Cora. That's not normal. I'm not sure what it is, but Freud would have a field day."

"Yeah, but he's dead. Like Hank. I wonder if Freud ever robbed a liquor store."

"Hank Wells really robbed a liquor store?"

"It's a good bet. He bought an Iron Man mask, and he didn't want anyone to know."

"According to Sergeant Crowley's girlfriend."

"Yeah, but you can take it to the bank."

"You trust her that much?"

"No, but it's a million-to-one coincidence she made a detail like that up."

"I suppose," Becky said. "Well, it's a good thing you didn't tell Crowley. He'd have told Chief Harper."

"Oh."

Becky's eyes widened. "You *told* Chief Harper!"

"I didn't tell him about Crowley's girlfriend. Or questioning the witness. Or the Iron Man mask. I didn't really tell him anything. I just told him he could go on the assumption Hank Wells robbed the liquor store."

"Oh, great," Becky said sarcastically. "Just that one minor detail." Her eyes widened. "Hey! Wait a minute! You saw Chief Harper *before* you saw me?"

"I thought if I saw you first you'd tell me not to do it."

"I *would* have told you not to do it."

"See?"

"Cora. You're on my side. You can't go running to the cops with everything you get."

"That's why I didn't give them everything I got. There's two cops: Crowley and Chief Harper. I could have told them both everything. Instead, I told *one* of them *one* thing. I think that shows admirable restraint."

"That's all you told Harper?"

"Well, he asked me where the money from the robbery was."

"I suppose you told him it was paying my retainer."

"No, I told him it blew up."

Becky considered that. "Interesting idea. Why would Hank Wells rob a liquor store?"

"See," Cora said. "That's the question Chief Harper needs to answer. Instead he's all hung up on where I got the idea. Because I was a good girl and didn't tell him how I got the idea."

"You're a saint. Why *did* Hank rob the liquor store?"

"Best guess he wanted some money his wife didn't know about."

"Why did he need it?"

"Because he didn't expect to blow up."

"Obviously, but what *did* he expect?"

"If we knew that, we might know who killed him. There's just one problem with that."

"What?"

"If he was trying to squirrel money away from his wife, as a suspect she's starting to look awful good."

Becky considered that.

"You gonna tell her about this recent development?" Cora asked.

"I don't know how she'd react to it."

"I do. If Hank robbed a liquor store, she'd want you to get the money."

"That's not funny."

"You just have no sense of humor. You gotta lighten up, Becky. Want me to get you a California bun?"

Becky leveled her finger. "Don't you dare. I had a dream about California buns."

"So what do you want me to do?"

"I want you to do the job you failed to do so far."

"Wow! Are you bending over backward *not* to treat me with kid gloves because I'm flipping out over a cigarette?"

"Right," Becky said. "I'm not *really* upset about you running to Chief Harper; it's all just a show."

"I was sure it was," Cora said. "So what's the job I failed to do so far?"

"Find the woman. Hank Wells' girlfriend."

"Rodney Klein says there wasn't one."

"And he's the best source of the information? What is he? Hank's golfing buddy? His best man? They grew up together?"

"Okay, who do *you* think is the best source of information on the subject?"

"How about the woman he was actually seeing?"

"Crowley says she's not the one."

"You didn't trust Crowley's opinion about the coworker. Why do you trust him on this?"

"The coworker acted guilty."

"Did this woman act guilty?"

"I haven't seen her."

"Aha!"

"You know," Cora groused. "I liked it a lot better when you were just feeling sorry for me."

Madeline Greer's eyes widened in surprise. "You're the Puzzle Lady."

Cora Felton smiled. "That's right."

"I can't talk to you."

"I beg your pardon?"

"I know why you're here. About the Hank Wells case. My lawyer said not to discuss it."

Cora smiled again. "Your lawyer said not to discuss it with the police. I'm not the police."

"You work with them. I've seen you on TV. Talking about the case. Well, not this case. But other cases. And you're always working with the police trying to prove someone guilty. My lawyer mentioned you specifically. Said not to talk to you."

"About the case, sure, I understand that," Cora said. "That doesn't mean we can't chat."

"Yes, it does. He said you're very smart and you'll find some way to turn it for your own purpose."

"Your lawyer flatters me. I'd put that on my Web site, if I had a Web site."

"You don't have a Web site?"

"I don't know how to make one. If I did, I'd just get e-mails with questions about crossword puzzles."

"You don't want to talk about crossword puzzles?"

"You ever go up to a doctor at a cocktail party and try to tell him your symptoms?"

"No."

"Well, trust me, he won't be happy. That's why I wasn't thrilled about the crossword puzzle you got."

"What do you mean?"

"What made you think it was for me?"

"I never said it was for you."

"The police seemed to think so. You must have told them something."

"No, I didn't. I— See? This is what my lawyer said you'd do. You're getting me to talk. And it's not fair. I have nothing to do with this. I just want to be left alone."

"If you have nothing to do with this, why do you need a lawyer?"

She smiled, shook her head. "No. You're very good, but you're not drawing me in. I talk to you and the next thing I know I'm in the *New York Post*. I don't want my name in the paper. I just want to be left alone."

"It's not that bad," Cora said.

Madeline stood blocking the door and stared Cora down.

"Okay," Cora said. "If you change your mind, you can contact me through my Web site."

"I thought you didn't have a Web site."

"I don't."

Cora went outside and stood in the street not far from where she had staked out the place to watch Hank Wells go in. Things had seemed so promising then. She'd tracked the guy to his love nest, found the other woman. Only she wasn't the other woman. She was just another dead end.

Cora heaved a sigh.

Okay, that didn't work.

Plan B.

Stephanie was incredulous. "You want me to do it again?"

"Not again. This is entirely different."

"How is it different?"

"You're not going to seduce anyone."

"I didn't seduce what's-his-face."

"No, he stopped short of renting the room. But you got him interested. You don't have to get this girl interested. Unless you're into that sort of thing."

A customer came in. Stephanie greeted him, listened to what he had in mind, set him up browsing samples on her Web site.

Stephanie returned to Cora, lowered her voice. "Just what is it you hope to accomplish?"

"Well, I don't expect a signed confession. But anything pointing in the direction of the killer would be appreciated."

"Specifically, what did you have in mind?"

"Specifically, what we were after before. Hank Wells' girlfriend. Crowley thinks this girl isn't it. He might be right. On the other hand, he wouldn't be the first man ever deceived by a woman."

"That's an interesting choice of words," Stephanie observed dryly.

"Let's not get sidetracked. If Crowley's wrong, I wanna know it. You would seem to be the authority on that subject."

The customer nodded his thanks and left.

"Think you blew a sale," Cora said.

"It's worth it if I can solve your problems."

"Was that sarcasm?"

"Perish the thought." Stephanie cocked her head at Cora. "So, can I take this all at face value?"

"What do you mean?"

"You're still trying to ace me out with Crowley, aren't you?"

Cora shook her head. "That ship has sailed."

"You'd say that even if you were."

"Probably. That's not the case."

"This isn't some clever ploy to get me to do things behind his back and then expose me so he thinks I betrayed him?"

"Hadn't thought of it, but that's a great idea."

"Cora."

"Relax. You're playing cop. What's the worst that can happen?"

"I get arrested and Crowley picks me out of a lineup."

"You're full of good ideas. Trust me, that's not gonna happen."

"What is?"

"Nothing. You're gonna interview a woman, ferret out her deepest, darkest secrets, and leave in a cloud of dust. Besides, it's something you're good at. Dealing with the other woman."

"Wow. Talk about a left-handed compliment."

"Okay, that was catty. But here's the thing. I got a client on the hook for murder. You haven't met her, but she's just the type of megaslut with no redeeming features outside of being young, dumb, and clueless, which, I don't have to tell you, appeals to more men than the law should allow. I'm so tempted to do nothing and let her fry that I'm bending over backward to save her."

"Do you really mean that, or is that a clever ploy?"

"Wow. I like the way your mind works. Is that result of living with Crowley?"

"I don't exactly 'live' with Crowley."

"You're just around."

"Yeah."

"Was he always this hard to get along with?"

"No. He's mellowed."

"That's frightening."

"Yeah." Stephanie took a breath. "Suppose I agree to do this. Specifically, what do you want me to get out of this woman?"

"Is she the girlfriend? If not, does she know the girlfriend?"

"Why don't you do it yourself?"

"She didn't want to talk to me."

"Will she want to talk to me?"

"No."

Stephanie considered. "Sounds like fun."

Madeline Greer came out the front door and headed for Broadway.

"That's her," Cora said.

Stephanie slipped out of the passenger seat, hurried across the street. She followed the woman to Broadway, caught up with her on the corner.

"Madeline Greer?"

"Yes."

"May I speak to you? It's rather important."

"What about?"

"Publicity."

Madeline put up her hand. "I don't want any publicity."

"Maybe not, but you're going to get some. You're about to be featured in an article about Hank Wells. I can stop it."

"What's this all about?"

Stephanie pointed to a diner on the corner. "Let me buy you a cup of coffee."

They sat at a booth and ordered coffee. Stephanie shrugged off

her coat. Her hippie garb was accentuated with beads and brace-
lets. All she lacked was flowers in her hair.

"*The Village Voice* is doing an article on the death of Hank Wells.
Part of it's about you."

"How do you know what's in the article?"

"Because I'm writing it."

Madeline sprang to her feet. "Get away from me!"

"Relax. I'm here to help you. I don't want to use you in the story.
I will try very hard to leave you out. But I'm short of material and
I'm getting pressure from the editor. If you will talk to me, *off the
record,* and give me a few leads, I will leave you out of the article
entirely and not even mention your name."

"Can you do that?"

"I'm writing it. If I don't put you in it, you're not there."

Madeline thought that over. "Can I trust you?"

Stephanie smiled. "Are you assuming if you couldn't I'd immediately confess?"

"I guess that was stupid. I really hate all this."

"Try a few questions. If you don't like 'em, don't answer."

"Okay."

Stephanie sipped her coffee, waited until Madeline sat back
down.

"Did you know Hank Wells?"

"Not really. I barely knew his name."

"But he came to your apartment?"

"I'm not sure I should answer that."

"How did you meet him?"

"I needed insurance."

"You went to his office?"

"No. I called him on the phone."

"What did he say?"

"He said he was very busy, but he'd fit me in. He said he was
out all day seeing clients and he'd drop by."

"That didn't make you suspicious? Like he had some ulterior motive for seeing you at home?"

"Why? I called an insurance agency. I should be worried about the agent?"

"I guess not. And he sold you a policy?"

"We discussed the policy. He said he'd have to fine-tune it. Which was awfully nice of him. It wasn't very big."

"And that's the only time you saw him?"

"No. He came back to show me the revised policy. It wasn't really very different. I felt sorry he was going to so much trouble for something so small."

"So you bought the insurance?"

"No. I was about to sign. He found a typo that actually altered the meaning. He said he'd have to come back."

"Did he?"

She hesitated. "I don't think I should say any more."

Stephanie didn't push it. "Fine. You've been very helpful. I'll leave you out of it." She picked up the check, dropped money on the table. "Oh. Just one question. How did you get in touch with Hank in the first place? Did you just call the insurance company and that's who you got?"

"No. A woman in my Pilates class recommended him."

"Oh?"

"Yeah. I was talking about insurance, she said she knew just the guy."

"A good friend of yours?"

"No. Just a woman in the class."

"Does she work for the insurance company, too?"

"No."

"What does she do?"

"I don't really know her well." She frowned. "Her name's Wendy something. I don't think she ever said what she did. Oh, wait. Someone else said something. What was it now? Oh! That's right."

"What?"

"She's an oral hygienist."

Cora put up her hand to block the high-speed drill. "Touch me with that I'll break your arm."

The hygienist looked shocked. At least Cora assumed she looked shocked. Wendy Ross was wearing the surgical mask worn by all dentists, periodontists, and oral hygienists since the dawn of AIDS.

"You don't want your teeth cleaned?"

"Quick learner. Put down the drill."

"I don't understand."

"Okay, maybe I was too hasty with the 'quick learner.' Let's you and me have a little talk."

"But you made an appointment to have your teeth cleaned."

"Because you don't make appointments to have little talks."

"I'm going to get the dentist."

"It's a waste of time. He won't know."

"Know what?"

"How long have you been sleeping with Hank Wells?"

The face behind the mask froze. "Who are you?"

Cora smiled. "Thanks. I needed that. I was just getting frustrated with the price of fame and not being about to do anything myself. I almost sent Stephanie to see you. I figured it didn't matter if you recognized me."

"Who are you?"

"I'm not a star. I just get recognized. My name's Cora Felton. On TV I'm known as the Puzzle Lady." She frowned. "Would you mind taking off that mask? I can't tell if you're impressed."

"I'm going to get the dentist." She turned to the door.

Cora reached out, grabbed her by the arm. "That would be a very bad idea. If you don't talk to me, you'll have to talk to the cops. They won't make an appointment, and they won't sit here in your nice little dental chair. They'll drag you down to headquarters and question you there. What do you suppose the dentist will have to say about that?"

She turned back. "What do you want to know?"

"Take off the mask."

The hygienist reached up and pulled off the mask. Wendy Ross was an attractive young woman, not quite thirty. Despite the unpleasant uncertainty of her current situation, she had a spunky sexuality about her, sort of an intelligent version of Brittany.

"Hmm. Not bad. I can see why Hank would be interested."

"Well, you're way off base. Hank was just a patient."

"Got his teeth cleaned a lot, did he?"

"No. Not at all."

"Really? You know how often your name appears in his appointment book last month?"

"I know he was having some work done."

"One usually makes the appointments with the dentist, not the hygienist. Why is your name in the book?"

"I'm not responsible for what someone writes in their appointment book."

"I agree. And I think it's totally unfair of Hank to have put you in that position. Too bad we can't call him on it."

"Why are you being so awful? The man is dead."

"Sorry about that. I was trying to judge from your reaction how much he meant to you. Was he just a casual fling?"

"I was not involved with Hank Wells!" Wendy said. She realized she'd raised her voice. "What is this all about?"

"What do you think it's all about? The man's dead. We're trying to find out who killed him."

"I thought some guy confessed."

"Heard about that, did you? I wondered if you had."

"It was on the news."

"It was on the news in *Bakerhaven*. You get Connecticut Channel Eight?"

"It was on the news here."

"Right. And then Hank didn't show up for his 'appointment.' Tell me, when's your day off?"

"Why?"

"Hank may be kinky, but I can't imagine him doing it in this chair. I wonder how many of his appointments were actually on your day off. On second thought, get the dentist in here. Let's see how many of Hank's appointments were actually with him."

Cora started to get out of the chair.

Wendy put up her hands. "All right, look. I was seeing Hank. I'm really upset that he's dead. He did come to see me instead of the dentist. It wasn't always on my day off. Sometimes it was on my lunch hour. I don't want to be dragged into all this, and I certainly don't want to meet his wife. He's dead. None of this matters. Why can't you let it go?"

"That would be nice, wouldn't it? I can't do that. I got a job to do. I owe it to someone. Not his wife, she's an idiot. But this other woman."

"What other woman?"

"You wouldn't understand. But the good news is, I'm not the cops. And I'm not after you. I don't need to tell anyone about your tawdry little fling. Not unless I have to."

"I can't believe he wrote my name in his appointment book."

"He didn't. That was a bluff." Cora got up, pulled off the dental bib. "Nice job. My teeth have never felt so clean."

"Ever see the movie *Double Indemnity*?"

Brittany glared at Cora, looked over at Becky Baldwin. "Do I have to talk to her?"

"Yeah, you do."

"Why?"

"Because I'm your lawyer and you follow my advice."

"What if I don't want to?"

"You're free to hire another lawyer. You don't have any *money* to hire another lawyer, but you're free to do so. You may not like Cora, but she happens to be on your side."

"Why do I need anyone on my side? The case is over. The police know who did it. I don't see why you can't get them to release me."

"They can't release you," Cora said. "You're not in jail. They can drop the charges and she's working on it, but it involves legal procedures you need a third-grade education to understand."

"Are you going to let her talk to me like that?"

"Cora, behave. Brittany, shut up and listen. My God, it's like dealing with a kindergarten class. I'm your lawyer. There's some things I need to know. I need you to answer some questions. Cora's going to ask them. Try not to think about who's asking; just try to think of the answers."

"Why?"

"You want your money?" Cora said. "Then listen to your lawyer."

Brittany set her jaw.

"Excellent," Becky said. "Cora?"

"You ever see the movie *Double Indemnity*?"

"Why?"

"Oh, for Christ's sake!" Cora said.

Becky put up her hand. "Let us worry about what it means. You just worry about answering."

"Yeah, I saw it."

"When?"

"What difference—" Brittany stopped herself. "Sometime last month. It was on TV."

"Turner Classic Movies?"

"Huh?"

"Never mind. Why did you watch it?"

"What do mean, why did I watch it? It was on TV. I watched it."

"Did you watch it with Hank?"

"Yeah."

"It was Hank's idea?"

"Yeah. Hank wanted to watch it. Said it was a classic. But he didn't like it much."

"He didn't like it?"

"No. He said the guy in the movie was stupid. He should have known his wife was up to something when she and the insurance agent tricked him into signing that big policy."

"Oh, really? What would he have done any different?"

"He should have figured his wife was cheating on him. He should have hired a private detective to catch her at it."

"That's what he would have done?"

"Sure. He said if the guy had done that he'd be alive today." Brittany shrugged. "Well, not *today*. It's a pretty old movie, right?"

"Yeah," Cora said. "Pretty damn old."

Sergeant Crowley walked in the door to find Cora and Stephanie sitting together on the couch.

"Is this the threesome I've always dreamed of, or am I about to be whacked?"

"No reason we couldn't do both," Cora said.

"I'm off duty," Crowley said. "If I pour myself a jolt of whiskey, will you guys let me know what's going on?" He grabbed a bottle off the sideboard. "Anybody want one?"

"I'd kill for one," Cora said. "But no."

Crowley poured a tumbler of Irish whiskey, flopped in a chair. "What's going on?"

"How'd you like to do a little police work?" Cora said.

"I just poured a drink."

"I didn't mean now," Cora said.

"If you mean tomorrow morning, that's what I'll be doing. I'm a police officer. I have a job."

"I meant police work for me."

"Cora, since I've met you, it seems like nearly fifty percent of all my police work is for you."

"See?" Stephanie said. "I told you he wouldn't mind."

Crowley looked from one to the other. "You guys are ganging up on me? That doesn't seem right somehow."

"Oh, don't be an old grumpus," Stephanie said. "Wait'll you hear Cora's theory."

"Cora has a theory? I might have known."

"I think you'll like it," Cora said.

"I wouldn't bet on it," Crowley said.

"Hold your ridicule until you know what it is," Stephanie said.

"You mean it's that good?"

"No, it's that bad," Cora said. "But it will give you lots of ammunition to slam me with."

Crowley sipped his whiskey. "Okay, what's your theory?"

"It's a little complicated."

"Is it a little *convoluted*?"

"Very," Stephanie said. "But if you can't follow it, Cora can explain in words of one syllable."

"Okay. Give it a shot."

"Okay," Cora said. "Here's my theory. Brittany Wells did not kill Hank Wells."

"I thought that was pretty well established."

"Billy the Bug didn't kill him, either."

"Who did?"

"To reach that conclusion you have to understand the background."

"God save me."

"This whole thing started when Brittany Wells got it in her head Hank Wells was trying to kill her for the insurance money. She was way off base, of course. The insurance policy was on him, not her. Nonetheless, she became convinced he was having an affair. So she hired me and Becky to find out if it was true."

"It wasn't," Crowley said.

"Yes and no."

He frowned. "What does that mean?"

"He wasn't having an affair with the woman we thought he was. But he was having an affair."

"With who?"

"An oral hygienist named Wendy Ross."

"How do you know that?"

"Actually, Stephanie found out for me."

"What!"

"I hope you don't mind. It was something I couldn't do for myself, and as you keep pointing out, you have your own work. Anyway, Brittany wasn't entirely paranoid. Her husband *was* acting funny. And he really *was* having an affair.

"*And,*" Cora said, "guess how Brittany Wells got the idea in the first place? Watching *Double Indemnity* on TV one night."

"So what?"

"She watched it with her husband. It was his idea. And he pointed out how stupid the guy in the movie was not to hire a private detective to see if his wife was having an affair.

"So when Brittany becomes suspicious, as a result no doubt of clues carefully left for her—lipstick on a collar, or whatever other cliché telltale signs Hank comes up with—she goes straight to Becky Baldwin to see if it's true.

"So I enter the picture and follow Hank Wells to Madeline Greer. Only she's a dead end. At least that's your opinion, and you can't be wrong all the time."

"Is it necessary to beat me up, or is that just an added perk?"

"Sorry. Couldn't help it. Anyway, Madeline Greer is a dead end, at least from our point of view. Which doesn't suit Hank's plans any. She was meant to be the jackpot. To sell the idea, she's provided with a crossword puzzle, just in case her other qualifications in that department come up short. Now the stage is set for the money scene. Hank Wells is blown up in a car in broad daylight. It is supposed to look like he blew himself up accidently trying to rig a car bomb. Which might have worked, if remnants of the remote-control device hadn't been found in the wreckage. Now it's clearly murder, and Brittany Wells could have done it, despite the fact she was in the police station at the very moment the car blew up. Because otherwise she has a perfect alibi—she was in fear for her life, and she hired me to be her bodyguard. There I am, perfect patsy. The worst of which is I have to spend the whole morning with Brittany Wells at the mall."

"Wait a minute. You're saying you were hired to provide an alibi for Brittany Wells?"

"Exactly. Why else am I there? Like her husband's really going to kill her at the mall?"

"You're ratting out your own client? You're saying Brittany Wells set this up?"

"Just hear her out," Stephanie said. She shook her head at Cora. "I told you this wouldn't be easy."

"Yeah," Cora said. "Men never listen. Anyway, Hank is killed; the policy is found; lo and behold, it isn't on her; it's on him. Now Brittany can collect on the policy, unless of course she killed him. Which wouldn't have been a problem if the remote-control device hadn't been found. Now it's clearly murder, and Brittany stands to take the rap." Cora gestured with her right hand. "Enter Billy the Bug."

Crowley frowned. "I thought you said Billy didn't do it."

"He didn't. But if Brittany did, she doesn't collect. There's gotta be a fall guy. So Billy kills himself, after confessing by computer. *By computer,* for God's sake, instead of a signed suicide note? Of course they're a little more difficult to produce."

"You're saying Billy was murdered, too?"

"Of course. And the crimes are very similar."

"Similar?" Crowley said. "One's a firebombing and one's a hanging."

"But there is one glaring similarity. In both cases I am Brittany Wells' alibi. I am hired as her bodyguard, and I am with her at the time of the crime. In Hank Wells' case there was some wiggle room, thanks to the remote device. But in Billy's case there was no manipulating the time of death, no rigging an automatic hanging device. Brittany Wells couldn't have done it. She's innocent; Billy's guilty; she gets the money."

"So how did she do it?"

"She didn't. Brittany Wells is my client. Innocent as a newborn babe. And almost as intelligent."

Crowley tossed off his drink, reached for the whiskey bottle. "Okay, Cora. You told me how Brittany did it. Now you told me she didn't. I know you get a big kick out of withholding the punch line, but my patience is at an end. Tell me who did it, or I'm going to hit you with this bottle."

"Actually, it's fairly obvious when you consider Hank Wells robbed a liquor store wearing an Iron Man mask."

"What!"

"Chief Harper didn't tell you? That's because he has no proof. But, trust me, you can take it to the bank."

"I don't care. I'm in no mood to figure anything out. I wanna know who killed Hank Wells."

Cora told him.

Crowley came into the kitchen where Stephanie and Cora were making a fresh pot of coffee. "She's on the move."

"Now?" Stephanie said. "We ordered Thai."

"Call 'em back and cancel."

"It's too late."

"Is it really too late, or are you just saying that because you're hungry?"

"By the time we get done talking about it, it will be too late."

"Stephanie."

Crowley's cell phone rang. He flipped it on. "Yeah? . . . Okay, I'm on my way." He clicked it off again. "You girls stay and eat. I gotta go."

"Like hell," Cora said.

The doorbell rang.

"Oh, great," Crowley said. "We'll grab it on the way."

"You can't eat Thai food in a car," Stephanie said.

"Just watch me."

The three of them thundered downstairs, tipped the deliveryman, and picked up an order of pad thai, coconut-crusted shrimp, chive pancakes, and curry puffs.

Crowley's car was parked next to the fireplug out front. Cora hesitated before getting in.

"You sit up front," Stephanie said. "You're the detective. I'm the sidekick."

They got in the car and Crowley took off.

Cora turned around in the front seat. "You know the problem with this? I don't think there is a comic-book equivalent of our crime-fighting team."

"Isn't there Lois Lane and Lana Lang?"

"What, and he's Superman?" Cora scoffed.

Stephanie giggled.

"Must you?" Crowley said.

"Oh, shove a shrimp in his mouth," Stephanie said.

Perkins' voice crackled over the radio. "She's headed for the West Side Highway."

"If she's headed for Connecticut, you gotta call Chief Harper," Cora said.

"Thanks," Crowley said. "I never would have thought of it."

"Is he always this rude, or just when he has women to impress?"

"I wouldn't know," Stephanie said. "When I'm around, he's always trying to impress me. How's the shrimp?"

"To die for."

"Didn't I tell you. Want some pad thai?"

"Sure. They put in forks?"

"They put in one. We'll have to pass it around."

"They thought one person ordered all of this?"

The radio crackled. "She's taking the Cross County/G.W. Bridge exit."

"'Cross County' probably means Connecticut," Cora said.

It crackled again. "She's taking the bridge. Upper level."

"She's going to Jersey," Cora said.

"No kidding," Crowley said.

"You know anyone in Jersey?"

"Bruce Springsteen."

"He a cop?"

"Not that I recall."

Crowley picked up the phone and called the cops while Cora and Stephanie ate pad thai.

"New Jersey State Police."

"This is Sergeant Crowley, NYPD, following a murder suspect into your jurisdiction. I'm going to need backup to make an arrest."

"You want us to arrest a fugitive?"

"She's not a fugitive. This is not a high-speed pursuit. She's just a suspect in a murder."

"She's wanted for murder in New York?"

"Actually, it's a Connecticut homicide."

"I'll need authorization. Who's the Connecticut officer on the case?"

"The Connecticut officer is not with me. I have an eyewitness to make the ID."

"Who's the officer in charge? I'll give him a call."

"You can't call the officer in charge," Crowley said in exasperation. "This is not his surveillance."

"So you call him, have him authorize it."

"He won't authorize it."

"Why not?"

"Because he arrested someone else for the crime."

"Oh, for goodness' sakes!" Cora grabbed the phone from Crowley and launched into a two-minute tirade at the end of which the chastened New Jersey officer promised to get right on it and call back.

"My God!" Stephanie said. "I thought I knew every curse word in the book. But half of those I'd never heard before."

"I may have made 'em up," Cora admitted.

The radio crackled. "She's taking the Route Four exit."

"Copy that."

"'Copy that'?" Cora said. "Did you really say 'copy that'?"

"Haven't you ever been in a police car before?"

"You arrested me, if you'll recall."

"I didn't make the arrest."

"It was your case."

"Kids," Stephanie said. "Shouldn't you be telling the Jersey cops where we're going?"

"Not till I have to," Crowley said. "They're liable to swoop in and tip our hand."

"Yeah," Cora said. "Their idea of clandestine surveillance is probably with sirens and lights."

"Coming up on Seventeen, signaling for a right-hand turn."

"Maybe she's going to Ikea," Cora said.

"Oh, great. We could get some Swedish meatballs."

"She's taking Seventeen South."

"Damn. Looks like we're stuck with Thai."

Crowley swooped into the turn. Coming out of the loop, Cora could see Perkins' car up ahead. "There's Perkins."

"Yup. Can you spot our girl?"

"I'm sure you taught him well, so she's not in the car in front of him. And he'd want a good visual, so she's not in the same lane. Second or third car up ahead on the right fits the description."

Crowley clicked the radio. "Got you, Perkins. Which one is she?"

"Tan Prius two cars up in the right-hand lane."

"Do I get a gold star?" Cora said.

"No, Stephanie does."

"Why?"

"For not asking so many questions."

"Oh! Nice zinger. Score one for the sergeant. Too bad, though. I was about to give you a forkful of pad thai."

The right-hand signal of the Prius started blinking. They were coming up on a fast-food restaurant.

"If she drove all this way to go to Burger King, I'm gonna be pissed," Cora said.

"Oh the other hand, we could get a Whopper," Stephanie said.

"If you don't knock it off, it's the last time I take you girls anywhere."

"Oh, tough stuff," Cora said.

The Prius drove on by Burger King, pulled into the motel parking lot next door.

Perkins drove by and pulled into a mini-mall.

Crowley turned in to Burger King.

"Keeping her bracketed," Crowley said.

Cora nodded. "Old Indian trick. Can you say that anymore, or is it politically incorrect?"

"Probably," Stephanie said. "Everything else is."

The Prius pulled to a stop. Wendy Ross got out and knocked on the door of unit six.

Crowley whipped out his cell phone and called the cops. "Damn it!"

"What?"

"Got no cell-phone service." Crowley hopped out of the car and walked around the lot until he found a spot where his call went through. He was back in a minute.

"You get 'em?" Cora said.

"Yeah. They'll be here in fifteen minutes."

"We could get a pizza delivered sooner."

"Yeah, if we had cell-phone service."

"You gonna stop 'em if they leave?" Cora said.

Crowley shook his head. "I got no jurisdiction."

"I do," Cora said. She reached in her purse, pulled out her gun.

"Put that away," Crowley said. "Are you trying to get arrested?"

"No, I did that. It wasn't as much fun as I thought."

The New Jersey cops were there in the ten minutes. The officer in charge was young and chisel jawed with piercing eyes and rock-hard abs, just the type to take charge and challenge Crowley to a pissing contest.

The cop surprised her when he let Crowley explain the situation and said, "How you wanna play it?" Cora would have married him on the spot.

Crowley pointed to Cora. "This woman's an eyewitness. I thought she'd knock and say, 'Maid service.' When they opened the door we'd push in and make the arrest."

"And if they say, 'Go away; we don't need anything'?"

"We kick the door down or get the key from the manager."

He shrugged. "Works for me."

It worked for Crowley, too. Cora knocked and said, "Maid service," the oral hygienist opened the door, and the cops swarmed in and arrested the killer.

Hank Wells.

Chief Harper was on the phone when Cora, Crowley, and Stephanie came in. He acknowledged their presence with a nod and continued the conversation, his side of which consisted largely of saying "Uh-huh." Finally he hung up the phone. "That was Henry Firth. Becky Baldwin wants to know how he can justify charging her client with the murder of a man I currently have under arrest."

"Aw," Cora said. "Poor Ratface."

"It's not funny, Cora. You mind telling me what the hell happened?"

"The key was the dentist," Cora said. "The minute I knew Hank Wells' girlfriend was an oral hygienist, it all fell into place."

"All *what* fell into place?" Harper said. "I'm going to have to make a statement, and I don't know what I'm going to say. This would appear to be the most convoluted crime in history. That's from what I understand, and I don't understand much. You wanna fill in the blanks?"

"Was that a crossword allusion, Chief? You make too many

crossword puzzle allusions, people are going to think I solved the case."

"You *did* solve the case. I don't mind people knowing that. I *do* mind them knowing I don't know what the hell you solved."

"Hank Wells killed himself. At least he made it *look like* he killed himself." Cora frowned. "I don't mean he made it look like *he* killed himself. I mean he made it look like *someone else* killed him. First his wife, then Billy the Bug. See, this was a very simple crime dressed up as a very elaborate crime. And all because of the movie *Double Indemnity*. Which, by the way, Hank Wells watched with his wife on Turner Classic Movies."

"Is that important?"

"Actually, it is. The movie helped him commit the crime. At the same time, it forced him to dress it up with all these convoluted twists."

Harper turned to Sergeant Crowley. "You buy all this?"

"Yeah, I do. But only because I've had it explained to me. Even then it wasn't easy."

"It helps if you suspend disbelief. Not to mention reason and sanity," Stephanie said.

"Pardon me, but who are you?" Harper said.

"My biggest fan," Cora said.

"I'm Stephanie. Pay attention to the *Double Indemnity* bit, Chief. It's rather good."

"What about the movie?" Harper said.

"Hank watched the movie with his wife," Cora said. "He did it deliberately, and for a reason. To put the idea in her head that he intended to murder her for the insurance money."

"Why would he want to do that?"

"Because he wasn't planning to at all. And he wanted to make his wife look scatterbrained. Not that hard to do. He convinces his wife that he's having an affair, that he's insured her life for a million dollars and he intends to kill her for the money. That couldn't be further from the truth. Yes, he's having an affair, but the insurance policy isn't on her; it's on him."

"Why does she think it's on her?"

"Because he told her so. I don't know that, but just ask her. I'm sure he did. He said something like, 'Honey, I insured your life for a million bucks, but it's not nearly enough, because you're worth so much more to me.' Because it sounds better than, 'I insured your life for a million bucks so if you die young I'll be rich.' Anyway, she's cool with that until she sees the movie. And since she sees it with him, he's able to plant the seeds of doubt with a few choice comments. He also manages to sell the idea the guy was really stupid not to hire a private detective to see if his wife was having an affair.

"One problem with pretending to be dead, after you're dead you can't do anything that shows you're alive. And before you're dead you can't do anything that would tip off the fact that you were pretending to be dead. Hank's problem was money. They didn't have a lot. What they did have he couldn't really withdraw from the bank right before his supposed death. That would be just too big a clue.

"Enter Iron Man."

"Oh. He robbed the liquor store because he needed money," Harper said. "So he could hole up and pretend to be dead."

"Exactly," Cora said. "Anyway, he plants the idea of hiring a private detective. And Brittany snaps at the bait. There are no private eyes in Bakerhaven, but there is a lawyer. She hires Becky Baldwin to help her with the case. Becky hires me to do the legwork.

"Which is just what Hank's been waiting for. As soon as he spots me following him—which is not that hard to do when you're looking for it—he puts his plan in motion. The next day he calls Madeline Greer, who he's been stalling along about an insurance policy, and tells her he'll drop by with it. He gets off work and leads me right there.

"The apartment has a window on the street. He makes a point of looking out so I'll know which apartment it is. As luck would have it, Madeline appears in the window, completing the picture. And to make sure he sells it, a crossword puzzle shows up in her apartment."

"Hank left that?" Harper said.

"Of course he did. He knows I'm the detective on the case. If not, he's pretty sure whoever finds it will give it to me. This, of course, is in the event anyone tries to trace his back trail after his death. If so, it will lead to Madeline Greer, who happens to be a dead end. A carefully constructed dead end to keep anyone from getting on the real trail."

"Which is?"

"Wendy Ross. Hank's coconspirator, who's the one who sent Madeline Greer to Hank as part of a prearranged plan."

"This is where my eyes start to glaze over," Chief Harper said.

"That's too bad, because we've barely scratched the surface."

"Well, scratch it then. What is the point of all this?"

"To collect two million dollars in life insurance, of course. The problem in doing that is the movie, *Double Indemnity*. See how we keep coming back to it? Because of the movie *Double Indemnity*, you can't kill your wife for the insurance money anymore. The first person they look at is the husband. Hell, the *only* person they look at is the husband. That's the only person who benefits. It's kind of a no-brainer. Even the slowest cop can handle it."

"Thank you," Harper muttered.

"So, you wanna kill your wife for the insurance, you have to have a perfect alibi. Take this case, for instance. A car bomb. Sure, you could have a perfect alibi for the time of the murder, but it's a device *designed* to go off when you aren't there. The remote-control detonator is just the icing on the cake. It wasn't accidental; it was murder. In light of all that, how in the world can you pull it off?

"Hank Wells found a way. You don't kill your wife; you kill *yourself*. And why does that work when the other doesn't? The husband killing the wife would be *Double Indemnity* with the sexes reversed. The wife killing the husband is a perfect copy. So how can it possibly work? Easy. His wife is a moron. She's too stupid to commit the crime. Plus, she's told the policy is on her. It's a genuine shock when she finds out it's on him. It's not like she has to be an actress to pull it off. She really thinks it's true. And now you see the point of hiring me."

"I wish you hadn't said that," Harper said.

"Sorry. I'm hired as Brittany's alibi. After I find his make-believe mistress, Hank manages to give his wife the idea that he realizes he's been tailed and he suspects her of doing it. She's terrified, and, as could be predicted, hires me to keep her safe. Hank rigs a car bomb, and explodes it at a time she couldn't possibly do it. Which is crucial to the whole thing. She can't be found guilty of murder if she's going to collect on the insurance.

"Unfortunately, a piece of the detonator survives, suggesting the possibility she could have set it off by remote control. The worst of it is the detonator means it's not an accident: it has to be murder. So there has to be a murderer, and it can't be his wife. So, what can he do now?

"Naturally, Hank has been monitoring the case on television, and hears Rick Reed ask you about Billy the Bug."

"I said he had nothing to do with it," Harper said.

"It doesn't matter. His name was brought up as a suspect. His was the only name brought up as a suspect. He has a history of starting fires. Which offers Hank an out. Billy has to kill himself after confessing to the crime.

"A crossword puzzle sent to the police station says Brittany is innocent and suggests the existence of another killer. Brittany Wells *knows* there's another killer because she knows it isn't her. She's frightened into hiring me as a bodyguard again. So she'll have an alibi for the time of Billy's death in case anyone suspects it was staged.

"And right there you have the only similarity between the two crimes. One's an explosion; one's a hanging. One's supposed to look like an accident; one's supposed to look like a suicide. In both cases Brittany Wells has a perfect alibi and I supply it."

"Are you saying Brittany Wells is involved?" Harper said.

"Have you been listening? Brittany Wells has the IQ of a turnip. She could no more carry out a complicated plot than I could dance the lead in *Swan Lake*."

"Then I don't understand. Brittany winds up with the money.

Hank winds up a penniless fugitive, hiding out pretending to be dead."

Cora jerked her thumb toward the back of the police station. "You take a look in your holding cells lately?"

"What?"

"Wendy Ross. The woman you have under arrest for accessory to murder."

"What about her?'

"Take a look. See if you can't detect a certain resemblance to the fair Brittany Wells. I bet a good hair and makeup artist could work a little movie magic."

"You mean?"

Cora shrugged. "That's gotta be the endgame. Brittany inherits the money, goes off on a victory voyage. Comes back a little older, a little wiser, and with a new gentleman in tow. Most likely one with conspicuous facial hair."

"And no one's going to notice the difference? Or recognize Hank?"

"You're too literal, Chief. When I say 'come back,' I don't mean here. Bakerhaven has bad associations. Her husband blew up here. Of course she'd want to leave town.

"Enter Wendy Ross. The new and improved Brittany Wells. Who, by the way, was the key ingredient in the crime. Wendy Ross was Hank Wells' oral hygienist. Who worked of course for Hank Wells' dentist. After his 'death,' she replaced Hank's files with the dental files of the man he killed."

"Who was that?"

"I don't know. But he was most likely one of the dentist's other patients. Which would make switching the files so much easier. She had all the charts and X-rays. All she had to do was change the names. I would imagine the next patient who misses an appointment is probably dead. Pull his files, they'll turn out to be Hank Wells'."

Harper thought that over. "I'll be damned."

Cora, Crowley, and Stephanie came out of the police station. Rick Reed was waiting to pounce. He shoved a microphone in Cora's face. "Here's Cora Felton now. Miss Felton, you were just with Chief Harper. Is it true he has Hank Wells under arrest?"

Cora smiled. "You'll have to ask the chief. He'll be making a statement shortly."

They tried to move off, but Rick grabbed Crowley before he could make his escape. Rick failed to notice the look on the sergeant's face when he put his hand on his arm. "And here's Sergeant Crowley of the NYPD. Sergeant, do I understand Hank Wells was in New York City when you made the arrest?"

Crowley sized Rick Reed up coldly and considered the question. He nodded. "Yes."

"And there you have it," Rick said triumphantly. "A Channel Eight exclusive. Sergeant Crowley of the NYPD confirms that he arrested Hank Wells in New York City."

Crowley shook his head. "No."

Rick Reed, about to ask a follow-up question, did a classic double take. "I beg your pardon?"

"No, that's not true," Crowley said.

"You just said you arrested Hank Wells in New York City."

"No, you asked me if you *understood* that I did. I figured you probably did think that, so I said yes, that's what you understood. You happen to be dead wrong, but that's not my problem." Crowley smiled at the badly discombobulated newsman, said to Cora and Stephanie, "It's cold out here. You wanna get some coffee?"

"Oh, yes, Cushman's Bake Shop," Stephanie said as they walked down the sidewalk. "I hear Mrs. Cushman's scones are to die for."

"Well, you can get 'em any time you want," Cora said. "Mrs. Cushman can't bake a lick. Her scones come from the Silver Moon Bakery at One-oh-Fifth and Broadway."

"And she passes 'em off as her own?"

"A small deception," Cora said. "Hank Wells passed himself off as dead."

They went into the bakeshop. Crowley had black coffee. Cora and Stephanie had lattes and scones. They stood in the bakeshop window, looking out at the street.

"Hard to believe there was a car bomb there," Crowley said.

"Where was it?" Stephanie said.

"In front of the library," Cora said.

"Right across from the police station," Crowley said. "That was a stroke of bad luck. Brittany being in the police station at the time. Close enough to have set it off by remote control."

"Because they found a piece of the detonator. Otherwise, what better alibi witness than the chief of police?" Cora smiled. "I'll be sorry to see you kids go. You're the only other woman I've ever liked."

"I'm really not the other woman," Stephanie said.

"No, I am."

"Cora," Crowley said.

Cora put up her hand. "No. Don't spoil it. This is way too civilized. And frankly, it's been a lot of fun. You guys are good together."

"Cora," Stephanie said.

"Yeah, I know, you're not a couple, yada yada yada. Shut up and eat your scone, you skinny bitch. God, you thin women who can pack it away and not put on an ounce." Cora smiled. "Ah, that feels better. A cleansing breath of resentment. I'm back in my element."

Stephanie laughed. "Crowley was right. You're delightfully strange."

Sherry came in with Jennifer on her hip.

"Can walk!" Jennifer said indignantly.

"Of course you can."

Sherry put her down, and Jennifer wrapped her arms around Cora's leg. Cora tousled her hair. Sherry nodded hello to Crowley and Stephanie. "Everyone's outside the police station waiting on the chief. You got anything you can give Aaron?"

Cora looked at Crowley. "How about an exclusive with the cop who arrested a dead man?"

"Really? Great. I'll get him. Come on, Jennifer, let's get Daddy."

"I didn't really arrest him," Crowley said. "It was the Jersey cops' jurisdiction."

"You can clarify that in the interview. He can still use the headline. He'll write something like 'Sergeant Crowley was quick to point out . . .' It doesn't matter. Go. Go, you guys, do the interview."

"What about you?"

"I'm family. I'm taken for granted. The scoop is an exclusive with you."

Crowley and Stephanie went out. Cora watched them go, not without a twinge of regret. Life was full of disappointments. It hadn't seemed like so many when she washed them away with alcohol or calmed her nerves with a cigarette. Damn. Why did everything make her think of a cigarette? And she was putting on weight, which caused her anxiety and made her want to smoke. Should she have another scone? Of course she shouldn't. But these were stressful times. She'd been eating a lot. What difference could one scone make?

Or if she wanted to be really wicked . . .

Cora bought a California bun. She took a bite, and everything was all right with the world. Excellent decision! She could always diet tomorrow. Today was a day to celebrate.

The door banged open and a small whirlwind blew in. It was Brittany Wells, flush with triumph and high as a kite.

"Victory is mine!" she declared. "Freedom, redemption, money, money, money! It's double indemnity after all! If my husband gets the death penalty for the murder, that's accidental death! At least as far as the insurance company is concerned. When I get done testifying, he'll be lucky they don't fry him on the spot. Anyway, he's alive, so all his assets are unfrozen, and guess who's attaching them to pay for my legal fees? He's responsible for them, seeing as how they were incurred through his actions. I don't understand it all, but Becky does, and the money is mine!

"Anyway, she says I owe you big-time. I don't see it, but she says it's a deal breaker. If it weren't for you, none of this would have been possible."

Brittany reached in her purse, pulled out a folded paper. "She made me write you a check. It's excessive, but she was firm."

Brittany extended the check in Cora's direction, said, "Oops!," and dropped it on the floor. "Clumsy of me," she said, turned, and swooped out as briskly as she'd come.

Cora looked down at the folded check. She was tempted to let it lie. She humbled herself, bent down, picked it up, unfolded it.

It was for ten thousand dollars.

Cora's eyes misted over. Damn Becky. Becky knew she'd be depressed watching Crowley and Stephanie ride off into the sunset. As if money could cheer her up. The only satisfaction she'd get from the money would be depriving Brittany of it.

She was tempted to tear the check up.

"Miss Felton?"

Cora turned around.

It was Mrs. Wilson. The plump, matronly woman's eyes glistened with tears. "I can't thank you enough. You didn't think you could do it, but you did. Now everyone will know. Billy didn't kill anyone. He couldn't kill anyone. He was a kind boy, a gentle boy. He didn't kill that man. And he didn't kill himself. I knew he didn't. Now everyone will know he didn't. Thanks to you."

Cora's smile was forced. She didn't want the woman's thanks. Not when it was her irresponsible tip to Rick Reed that had dragged Billy into the case. Yes, she'd brought her son's killers to justice, but it wasn't enough. Nothing would ever be enough.

"I'm having a small memorial for him this weekend. I'd like you to come. If you would be so good. It would mean a lot."

"Of course."

Cora sighed as Mrs. Wilson went out the door. She'd have to go. It was the least she could do.

Chief Harper came in, spotted Cora. "Thought I might find you here." He pointed to the pastry in her hand. "What's that?"

"California bun."

"Is it good?"

"You don't want to know."

"Sounds irresistible."

Harper went up to the counter, bought a black coffee and a California bun. He took a bite. A change came over his face. "Oh, my God."

"Don't say I didn't warn you, Chief. Try not to eat more than three a day."

He took another bite, sipped his coffee. "I saw Mrs. Wilson going out. Did she hit you up?"

"For the memorial?" Cora said.

"Yeah. You going?"

"Yeah. You?"

Harper nodded. "She'd notice if I didn't. I'm the chief of police. And there won't be many people there. It's just a small ceremony. Not a church service. Poor woman. She'd have liked to give her boy a proper send-off, but of course she can't afford it."

Cora blinked. She smiled slightly.

Sometimes life's ironies, by pure chance, actually came up with the proper random sequence of events.

Brittany Wells' check was burning a hole in her pocket.

Cora pulled it out, unfolded it.

"As a matter of fact, she can."